M000190283

The Imagined Homecoming of Icarus Isakov

Copyright © 2019 by Lavender Line Press

All rights reserved. No part of this publication may be reproduced, distributed, or transmitted in any form or by any means, including photocopying, recording, or other electronic or mechanical methods, without the prior written permission of the publisher, except in the case of brief quotations embodied in critical reviews and certain other non-commercial uses permitted by copyright law. For permission requests, write to the publisher, addressed at the email below.

Lavenderlinepress@gmail.com

Ordering Information:

Quantity sales. Special discounts are available on quantity purchases by bookstores, corporations, associations, and others. For details, contact the publisher at the email address above.

Orders by U.S. trade bookstores and wholesalers may also order directly from Ingram Spark.

ISBN: 978-0-9981492-4-0

Hiraeth[1]

[hiraɪϑ, hi-raeth] *noun*, Welsh

A homesickness for a home to which you cannot return, a home which maybe never was; the nostalgia, the yearning, the grief for the lost places of your past.

---

[1] *other-wordly.tumblr*

An Unexpected Letter

I mean no offense, but your imagination has been poisoned by fairy stories. All the once upon a times, wicked witches, white knights, imprisoned princesses, prince charmings, spellbinding sorcery, spell-breaking kisses, poisoned apples, golden goose eggs, all those happily ever afters - they've convinced you that your shit doesn't stink, or if it does, that your fairy godmother will sprinkle sweet-smelling pixie dust on it. Allow me to decondition you from such fantastical malarkey. If I don't, I'm afraid you'll find this story impossible.

Consider the following.

Peter Pan grew up and into a director of commercial lending for the Royal Bank of Scotland. Bluebeard's beard was a highly average brown. After Dorothy returned from Oz, she overdosed on barbiturates. Sleeping beauty was only pretending to be asleep. Rip Van Winkle never woke up. The lost boys stayed lost. Cinderella was a gold-digger. Moses was high[2] on Mount Sinai. George Washington lied, plenty. The Virgin Mary was laid, obviously. Once upon a time never was. Happily ever after never is. You can't sing. Neither can I.

Don't get me started on supernatural stereotypes. Most of those are outright delusional. Vampires are not sexy. Vampires are scary. Ghosts? Not necessarily scary. I've never met a witch I didn't like. Wish I could say the same for wizards. Most wizards I know are elitist trolls. Real trolls, on the other hand, are among the most humane species on the planet. Werewolves make for great pets. Leprechauns are Dutch. Saint Nicholas is fit. Monsters don't hide under beds. They sleep in beds, just like you and me.

As for goblins, forget everything you've ever been told. It was rubbish of the most rubbishy sort. I should know. I am a goblin. Name's Icarus Isakov. I know what you're thinking, sounds more Greek than goblin. Rest assured, I *am* a goblin, and being a goblin, I am the foremost authority on all things goblin, so let me clear some things up about them, and me.

Goblins are more human than most humans. What I mean by that is we're more civilized. Take me, for example. I may not be the height of refinement, but I like to think of myself as a cultured goblin. I drink red wine. I read books. Sometimes, I drink red wine while reading books. Sometimes, I drink too much red wine while reading books.

---

[2] You know, high. On drugs.

I go to the theatre when I have money to go to the theatre, which is not often if I'm being honest. I eat only taco-shaped potato chips. I love documentaries. I avoid generic furniture and clothing. I am a vinyl music enthusiast. I meditate. Well, I try to meditate. I'm no Gandhi. Goblins can't sit still. We're too productive to sit still.

So, I'm sorry, but goblins don't have razor-sharp teeth for the devouring of human flesh. We don't have those lanky, gross-looking chicken legs and arms. No pot bellies. No beady, bloodshot eyes. No fungus-infested claws. In fact, goblins look rather unspectacular. Picture a coffee-colored hobbit with itty-bitty horns, and there you have yourself an ordinary goblin.

A few more points of clarification. We don't live in deep, dark caves under mountains, plotting the destruction of the free world. We are not malicious by nature. We don't own weapons for the butchering of dwarves and elves. I don't own any weapons, and some of my closest friends are dwarves and elves. I'm a good goblin, from a friendly goblin species.

There is the one stereotype I'll grant you, and that relates to goblins and mining. It's true, goblins mine. Today, goblins hold most of the few remaining jobs in the mining industry. I'm from a small ruby mining town myself. Rockville, it's called. It's more picturesque than it sounds. It sits in this deep, green valley, below snow-capped mountains with great green pine forests for beards. A wiggling river, clearer than a magic mirror, flows down from the mountains, encircling the town. The town itself was the epitome of quaint. Main Street ran through a dainty downtown, surrounded by patches of neighborhoods and farms.

Rockville was a nice place to grow up, but not to be a grown-up. I left town long ago. I went off to college. Had to. Mining was never a realistic career choice for me, or anyone else nowadays. My dad was a miner. I saw how his back curved, crooked as a cockatrice claw, before he was the least bit old. Mining is an honorable life, not a comfortable one.

School suited me right down to the ground. I liked learning. I earned myself the most practical of business degrees. I wanted to be one of those wise, well-dressed masters of the market. I can't complain about how that worked out. I landed a respectable banking job, then a proper place in the city. I'm living my best goblin life, and quite comfortably. I'm still a bachelor, with little responsibility beyond my monstrous mortgage. I have a good time; sometimes out with friends, sometimes home for a night of fine wine and literature. In either case, one thing is certain - I'm sleeping in. Sleep is shamefully underrated in this modern world.

You can count on one gnome hand the number of times I've been back to the sleepy small town of my youth over the past few years. The last time I was back was for the funeral of mom and dad. They died *Notebook* style, in their sleep, just days apart. They say when you're married forever, that's how you generally go.

For me, the town died when my parents did, though it had been sick awhile before then. The story of the town's downfall was an all too common one. Recession hit. Painkillers killing more people than pain. Progress passed the town by. Residents left for big city jobs. The coup de grâce was when the mine finally closed. One day, out of the blue, it ran out of rubies. Captain capitalism has no use for ruby-less ruby mines. That mine employed half the town. When it closed, the town closed with it. Some folks remained, either too old to leave, or too young to know any better, but most left.

With my parents and most of my friends gone, I had no real reason to return home. It was an awfully long drive through nowhere, and once I got there, I'd have nowhere to stay. So, the time passed, quickly as it tends to for a goblin. Weeks turned to months, months to years, and I never once returned. I wanted to remember Rockville as the happy-go-lucky town it was in my childhood, not the ghost town it had become.

Then, an unexpected letter arrived.

***

Late one morning, I was brushing the old goblin fangs, sifting through the mail. It started out a typical, worthless batch. Junk, junk, bill, junk, more junk. I'm one of those hopeless romantics, always on the look-out for that elusive personal letter, though it rarely comes. So, when I read her name on this small, scarlet envelope, I barfed a mouthful of toothpaste goop all over the bathroom mirror in astonishment. The sight of her name alone made me all weak and wobbly.

Ruby Rockhollow.

She was named after that precious gemstone, the lifeblood of Rockville, extracted from the mine since time immemorial. Ruby was precious herself. In some ways, she was the beating heart of the town. Everyone knew Ruby. You couldn't miss her. She was one of only a few humans in town, and a stunning sight at that. She was everything to everyone. She was the class president, homecoming queen, poet laureate, grand marshal, grand champion, and anything else you can think up. If Rockville had a royal court, she'd have been the princess.

For me, Ruby was the girl next door. I'd known her since before my horns sprouted. Growing up, we were pretty much inseparable. We walked to school, ditched school, hunted for lost treasure, got lost hunting for lost treasure, climbed up trees, rolled down hills, hunted bugs, caught fish, skimmed stones, dammed streams, and all the rest. We were best friends.

The nature of our relationship grew more complicated as teenagers. There were times we were friends, more than friends, not friends, then back to being friends again. High school was awkward for me, just like everybody else.

Competing for her attention was awful. I generally failed to get it. I was no match for the slack-jawed yokel's chasing her.

Not that I was a total zero. She was just a perfect ten.

We managed to stay close enough through those teenage years. I went away to college, and she stayed home, but we kept in touch, writing and calling, seeing each other when I came back home. I moved away just after graduation. After that, it only took a couple of years to lose touch completely. I can't say how, or exactly when we lost touch. It just happened all mysterious-like, how it always does. Before I knew it, I'd not seen or heard from Ruby in years.

About a million questions raced through my head as I opened the letter. What could she possibly be writing for? Was she single? Any kids? How had she found my address? Why was there no return address? Why doesn't anyone write letters anymore? What is a scarlet letter, anyway? Sounds vampirish. Do Jewish vampires avoid Christian crosses? And so on.

The letter raised more questions than it answered.

Dear Icarus,

I came over to your house today, but no one was home. I figured you'd be somewhere around the neighborhood, but you were nowhere around the neighborhood. I looked everywhere for you - up in the treehouse, down at the park, up and down Main

Street. I saw your dad at the mine. He didn't know where you were either. I walked all the way across town through the woods to the river, thinking you might be fishing, or swimming. I walked far along the river, then farther, closer to the mountains. I went so far, I went and got myself lost in the summertime, without the time part. Are you lost too? If so, we should be lost together. Wouldn't that be fun?

> *The rose is red*
> *The violet blue*
> *Dream a dream*
> *Of me and you*

> *Disrespectfully Yours,*
> *Ruby Rockhollow*

Ruby signed the letter in ruby red ink, the way she always did. Her signature was about all that made sense from the note. Why was she looking for me? Why would she come by my house, when I hadn't lived there in years? No one had. She claimed to have seen my dad at the mine. My dad had been dead, and the mine closed, for years. It made no sense for her to be searching around town for me when she knew damn well I was gone. Everyone was gone from that town.

THE IMAGINED HOMECOMING OF ICARUS ISAKOV

I didn't know what to make of the letter. It was like she'd written it years ago when we were still kids. It would have made sense then. Now it made no sense.

Stranger than the letter was the fact it came when it did. The old town had been on my mind. I'd been having these dreams of my childhood. They washed ashore randomly in the middle of the night, these little remembrances in a bottle, set adrift by who or what, I had no idea. In the dreams, I'd find myself somewhere familiar, somewhere I'd grown up like a backyard, playground, pool, or school hallway. I was always alone, always wandering through wherever, frantically searching for something, or someone who I could never find. Maybe I was looking for Ruby. Clearly, she was looking for me.

It was time to return home.

Nowheresville

Turns out it's hard to get back home when you left so long ago. There *was* once a train. I was born on that train, on a day so hot the train tracks melted into spaghetti. The train stopped, unable to ride along the noodles. Mom went into labor and, with nowhere to go, had me right there in the center aisle of the passenger car. When she found out the train was stopped due to what the conductor called "sun kinks" in the tracks, she named me Icarus. Growing up, she told me I fell straight from the sun one summer afternoon, right into her lap.

That train ran through our little mining town before it was the middle of nowhere because you can't be the middle of nowhere with a train running through town. The train was essential to Rockville. It brought townsfolk, industry, growth. It brought the world and took us to the world.

I'd intended to ride the train home, assuming trains never stop running. Wrong. Closed years ago, probably not long after the mine. No train was problematic. I couldn't drive home. Never much liked driving, so never owned a car.

I couldn't boat there. Town was landlocked. There was only one way for me to get home, and that was by airship.

There's only one type of airship that flies to the middle of nowhere, and that is an airship for-hire. Airships for-hire are raggle taggle contraptions; part pirate ship, part hot air balloon, entirely dangerous. They operate like flying carpools, taking groups of budget-sensitive passengers with a high accidental-fiery-death-by-airship-crash risk tolerance, to any number of remote destinations which lie in the same vicinity.

The airship I rode home looked like the Mayflower, but with more holey sails and less holy passengers. The captain looked like One-Eyed Willy. He looked too old to be commandeering himself, let alone an airship. The passengers were mostly goblins because we were flying over goblin country. There was a scattering of others - some trolls, orcs, a few pipe-puffing druids. The druids were high as the hills before we'd even lifted off.

We left late one afternoon, expecting to fly all through the night and arriving early the following morning. The ride was surprisingly smooth. Our elderly master and commander's bony hands at the wheel, navigating with one eye better than most would with three. I spent most of my time on deck relaxing, watching the world above and below, wondering about Ruby, Rockville, and what had become of it all.

Like most, I always had a love/hate relationship with

the place I grew up. We love our hometowns for all there is to love about childhood. We love them for all the friends, fantasy, first dates, and kisses. We hate our hometowns for the inevitable realization those things all go away, so we get it in our heads we too must go away. We leave home, hoping to find more of that raw stardust. And we do find it. But, just like when we were young, it soon fades away, and when it does, we wonder why we ever left home in the first place.

Ruby was one of those mystifying ones who never left home. I was always baffled at that. She could have gone anywhere, done anything, been anyone. Why stay? Maybe something kept her there. A job? Not many of those. Perhaps some special someone? Not many of those either. Maybe she just liked it in Rockville. Maybe she loved it. I'd once loved it long ago. The town loved me back then. I wondered if it still would. I wondered if it would even recognize me.

I looked out into the distance, out where the sun had just fizzled from something to nothing. A mess of clouds congregated over the last of the light. They were the first clouds I'd seen all day. In them, I saw the shapes of town as I remembered it. I saw rocking horses rocking, cream soda creaming, the pale shadows of kids racing, massive miners beating forth clouds of white smoke with puffy pickaxes. The whole downtown floated above me like a small-town heaven. Through the last shafts of daylight, little pink clouds swung their hips like cheerleaders. They danced on the horizon line to The Drifters, playing from the captain's static-filled radio.

There goes my baby, movin' on, down the line.

Wonder where, wonder where, wonder where she is bound?

I nodded off, Ruby among the cheerleaders swaying me to sleep. In the morning, I would be home. I wondered if I'd see her then.

***

I woke up with my neck in my stomach.

It was the angle of the airship. We were soaring what seemed like straight down, to what seemed like certain death. Goblins piss their pants like anyone, and I was about to unleash a torrent, when I noticed One-Eyed Willie. I assumed he had either abandoned the ship, or died of old age. I was relieved to find him standing calmly behind the wheel, wind blowing back his white locks. He winked at me before straightening the ship out.

"Next stop, Nowheresville," the captain croaked.

He brought the airship down into the arms of the mountains, just outside of the downtown, on Main Street. There was no one awake to notice us land. It was still too early, just before sunrise. The blue sky had only just started to drown out the stars. I grabbed my pack and hurried down the rope ladder from the side of the ship, glad to be off it. Instead of heading down Main Street, I sidetracked through my old neighborhood. I wanted to see my old house before I saw anything. Ruby had once lived next door. Maybe there'd be some sign of her there.

My house wasn't far. I only had a few blocks to walk, blocks that were once considered the swankiest in town, but now I found most of the houses abandoned, and that broke my goblin heart because I'd known all these houses and all the families in them. The Steelman's was hardly recognizable, suffocated under every species of plant imaginable. There was the Silverfox's, likely now home to actual foxes. It looked like someone maintained the old Pinkmoon place. Funny, because the Pinkmoon place was never maintained by the Pinkmoon's. Hopleaf house looked to have been mysteriously vaporized. Rockhold's was a pile of rocks. And on, and on.

Walking down my block was like walking through a still life painting - the most depressing one ever painted. Not a light flickered, not a car parked, not a creature stirred. My own house looked like a haunted house. It was half-covered in wild ivy, the other half what remained of the original brick, all weathered and crumbled, mortar gone. The chimney had collapsed on itself. Roof caved in. The sun rose, shining through the shattered front window, where I found myself looking for some sign of my parents. I half-expected to see them waltzing through the living room. Maybe mom would see me and come out on the doorstep, hands on her hips, smile on her face, waiting for me the way she used to after school. But school was out, and she was gone. Everyone was gone.

The girl next door was gone. You'd have thought a jumbo jet crashed into her house, the way it had crumbled into a trillion tiny bits. The only bit of Ruby left were her little handprints, sculpted into the wet driveway concrete long ago, when she was still a girl. I peered through the rubble into her backyard. She had this treehouse back there. We were always up there. It was like our headquarters. Incredibly, the treehouse was still intact.

I walked back to where the airship had dropped me off for a stroll down Main Street. I'd get the full story there. The story of every small town is written down Main Street. It's written in the forever broken streetlight, the Saturday night skid marks, even the individual cracks of the asphalt have a tale to tell. Every autumn, the homecoming parade marched down Main in all its glory and told our story. It was a proud story then. Now, it looked more tragedy than anything.

Main Street was open, though most everything on it was closed. The buildings sat abandoned, shutters across old familiar storefronts –Al's Grocers, the Corner Candy Shop, Movie Theatre on Main, whatever that diner was called. All closed. The roller rink looked to have burnt to the ground. The Rockville Reader, our local newspaper, was abandoned. No news to report, I guess. Christ, even the gas station had closed. If you can't sell gas in town, what the hell *can* you sell? Nothing was familiar. I may as well have been on Mars. Less than a handful of businesses opened for the day, which worried me. My stomach growled. Would I, could I find a coffee?

I would. The prehistoric corner drug store, stalwart supplier of the standard, remained. I beheld the rusty *Rexall Pharmacy* sign dangling from a steel thread and finally felt just a little bit home. The old store was old when I was young. Now it was ancient and, apparently, immovable.

I had a soul-saving coffee and donut breakfast inside the drugstore, at one of those old-fashioned soda fountain bars. I passed most of the day drugging myself inside the drugstore with copious amounts of caffeine and baked goods. The clerk didn't mind my loitering. Not like he was busy. I asked around for Ruby and other old friends, without much luck.

I wandered out of the drugstore, through downtown, closer to the woods and mountains toward the outskirts of town, where I noticed something strange. There was a new castle nestled into the mountainside. It wasn't big. It wasn't small either. It was more high than wide. Must have cost a fortune to build up there. They'd cleared half a forest to build it, and then there was the actual building of it. I wondered what sort of masochist would build a kingly castle in a cursed town.

I spent more time wandering around, wondering. I wondered if my return home was a mistake. The town didn't feel like home anymore. There was no sign of Ruby. Maybe there was nothing left for me in Rockville. The town wasn't just empty, there was a hollowness to it, like a rotted-out tree trunk. All I could find were dead roots, but I'd heard somewhere it took roots years and years to die. I held out hope for some stubborn old roots.

At sunset, I set off toward the edge of town, where a guest room awaited.

The Rockville Reader

Homecoming Parade Dazzles Down Main

On Friday afternoon, the annual homecoming parade, sponsored by your very own Rockville Masonic Lodge, dazzled its way down a crowded Main Street, continuing a generations-old tradition beloved by all.

Every year, you can expect the whole town to either march in the parade or watch it, and this year was no different. Lawn chairs, blankets, and coolers dotted the parade route all morning long. By the time the fun started late that afternoon, every soul in town was lined up along Main Street, from the high school to city hall.

You could feel the excitement in the air when the lights of Sheriff Griffin's cruiser appeared in the distance, signaling the start of the festivities. Mike "the Manticore Mechanic" Masterson sputtered by in his refurbished Model-T, candy flying out the windows and into the hands of the littlest (and quickest) ones. Our own district champion high school marching band followed, always the sight to see in formation. Honorable mention to the tuba player for keeping *pace in the heat! The varsity cheerleaders looked more comfortable in the bed of their pickup truck. The Centaurian Society galloped by, pulling Mayor Mandrake and family in a cleverly designed mine trolley float. Speaking of miners, the Future Miners of Rockville won the hearts and stomachs of all with their portable snow cone machine. The homecoming court, dressed to the nines in their evening gowns and dinner suits, looked resplendent under the fading afternoon sun. Sitting with poise in their folding chair thrones, waving down gracefully to the lines of parade goers below, they looked like the finest kings, queens, dukes, and duchesses in all the realm.*

Last came one Ruby Rockhollow, this year's honorary grand marshal. At just five years old, she's not only the youngest, but the grandest grand marshal this grizzled journalist can remember. Ruby was mounted on an immaculate feathered unicorn, compliments of Doolan's Stables. She trotted down Main like a seasoned equestrian, charming the crowd in a white sundress dotted with twinkling red rubies, carrying a bouquet of sweetheart roses. All cheered when she rode by.

A hearty congratulations to Otto "the only ogre in town" Ofenlock, winner of this year's watermelon eating contest. Another congratulations to Pat "Blackie" Lyons, on winning the parade raffle. Enjoy that free oil change Blackie!

Homecoming is a special time of year. It's a time for all us townies, from goblins to golems, to rally together. It's a time to celebrate our way of life, our families, and our kids. It's a time to fight, to win. It's a time to dance. Most importantly, it's a time to come home again. And in the words of someone wiser than I; home is more than just a place, it's a feeling.

Welcome home, Rockville.

The Forgetful Faun Inn

~ Tomorrow is not welcome today ~

Read a tattered, wooden signpost outside my home for the week, The Forgetful Faun Inn. I felt more like a yesterday. The whole town did.

The Inn sat strangely alone, a mysterious citadel on a grassy hill at the edge of town. This needle of a stream ringed the base of the hill, as though a giant had stood above the Inn and pissed himself a neat circle around it. On top of the hill, set against the night sky and shadowy mountains, candle-lit windows shone like cheerful beacons. The place was busy. I could see the smoking, dancing, and drinking silhouettes in the windows. Made me want to smoke, dance, and drink. I sped walk up the narrow, rocky path to the front door.

A quaint, two-story red brick cottage I might've mistaken for an ordinary house were it not for the plaque above the door, swinging gently in the wind, which read "Holy Grail Ale." Sounded mystically delicious. Strings of ivy reached up each side of the brick near the front door like green sideburns. I could hear chatter and music from inside.

Walking inside, I was pleasantly surprised at how pleasant it felt, especially compared to the rest of the town. Dimly lit, mostly from a candle wax drenched chandelier overhead and smaller lamps on each of the tables, the place was comfortably full of folks – goblins mostly, but also a scattering of humans, dwarves, and others. A stone fireplace crackled and popped, burning a woodsy scent. Drinkers drank at a snug bar glowing faintly from the firelight dancing in the funhouse mirror behind it. A group of folks crowded around the front window in conversation. One couple played darts in a corner. Another kissed in a different corner. Others talked, laughed, and danced. A piano player played for all of them, and tips. It was my sort of Inn. Little did I know, it was a different kind of Inn, pouring a different sort of spirit.

Looking around, I didn't see any obvious person or place to get the key to my room from, so naturally headed to the bar. Figured I'd have a drink and a chat with the bartender.

"Refreshment, to refresh your memory?" The bartender asked as he clip clopped over to me.

The bartender was a faun. He was dressed in a plain white t-shirt and jeans, devilish horns protruding out the front of an old, worn down baseball cap. He had the familiar face of an old friend. Not that he was all that old, or a friend. There was something else about him, something subtly sorcerous.

"Any specials?" I doubted out loud.

"Old Fashioned is. Always is. Didn't you know?" He looked at me funny. "This is a pub of the past. We are a remembrance racket, purveying only the finest, the most vivid in days gone by. Now then, one more time. Refreshment to refresh your memory?"

His answer, and second offer of a refreshment to refresh my memory left me confused. A drink to remember? Weren't drinks to forget? My mind wandered from confused to curious. I wondered what your run-of-the-mill memory tasted like. I decided to play along, though I wasn't sure of the game. My memory could use some refreshing, after all.

I asked the bartender for something I'd forgotten, something sweet, from when I was just a wee goblin. He pulled a tiny beige thing wrapped in clear wax paper from under the bar, handing it to me with a mischievous smile. The familiar scent overwhelmed me the instant I opened it. It was a glob of fresh cookie dough. My favorite, and I was more than a little unsettled at how the bartender knew it. I remembered licking this stuff off mixing spoons and spatulas as a kid. Being a memory, I felt less guilty eating it than if it were ordinary cookie dough.

The cookie dough had the intended effect, tasting sweet as it ever had, every bit as perfect as it was when I was young. I chewed and chewed the sticky goo, eyes closed, the side profile of mom in our galley kitchen reappearing in my mind, then melting away, along with the dough in my mouth.

Opening my eyes and staring into the funhouse mirror, I looked more alien than goblin. I looked younger. I stuck my brown tongue out, scrunched my nose, and made obnoxious faces. That felt good. I made a mental note to eat raw cookie dough more often.

I ordered another memory from the bartender. He gave me a handful with a wink. Turning around, looking at each of the individual patrons, I noticed something unusual. No one was staring zombie-like into a phone or computer screen. There was no head down. No selfies. In fact, there were no televisions, videos, or electronics of any kind, anywhere. Everyone was looking and talking to one another, instead of machines. They all appeared happier because of it.

Looking around, it didn't take me long to notice something else unusual. I saw a walking, talking grandfather clock, near the fireplace. He was tall and thin, with stringy arms and legs. He looked drunk as ever, swaying wildly here and there, always seeming about to fall, yet miraculously never actually falling. I walked over, joining the crowd of on-lookers. "The Tipsy Timepiece," they called him. Someone asked him the time, and he started ranting.

"*Of course,* I'd need a mirror to tell, what with the time *literally* being on my face! I now pronounce you past and present, and I pronounce myself wasted. Did you know, there is nothing so common in this world as wasted time? Time is wasted all the time. We waste time, then time wastes

28

us. Don't believe me? Then don't. But remember, I *am* the supreme authority on time within this establishment, being the only clock!"

Not how I pictured a grandfather clock behaving.

The drunken clock straightened himself out and cleared his voice. The crowd grew silent as he recited the following.

Once upon a time there was a never fairy named Hank

Cast under a pixilated spell from the whiskey he drank.

After one too many sherries

He slurred, "I don't believe in fairies."

Then fell into Mermaid Lagoon, where like a stone he sank.

There was a long and loud applause.

I found a little table to sit down at, set against a wall of bookshelves. Looking the titles over, it dawned on me these were no ordinary books. These were books I'd once read, but forgotten long ago. I saw familiar titles like, *Aesop's Fables, There Was an Old Lady Who Swallowed a Fly,* and *The 500 Hats of Bartholomew Cubbins.* I excitedly pulled down *A Light in the Attic* and skimmed through the pages, fondly remembering the weirdness within. Reading books in a bar was a first for me, but I couldn't resist. I sat there, chewing memories from the bar, reminiscing with each page.

Once I'd had my fill of Uncle Shelby, I found myself back at the forgotten bookshelf. *In Search of Lost Time* caught my eye from too high above to reach. I had this tall dryad drink of water snag it for me and started skimming through the pages. I'd forgotten the story almost entirely, but happened on one passage that stood out from the rest, "If a little dreaming is dangerous, the cure for it is not to dream less, but to dream more, to dream all the time."

I wondered if all those lost dreams might be found. The Inn specialized in memories. Dreams were a sort of memory. Some stay a little while, while others are gone in an instant. What about those elusive dreams - poof, gone like magic, the moment you wake? What if I could suddenly remember all those? Maybe, the best of all my memories were forgotten dreams.

I was on my way back to the bar to order a dream when the room suddenly quieted. I stopped, scanning the place, and noticed why. The piano player had stopped playing. He puffed a cigarette near his piano as he peered curiously out into the night through a window. I walked over. Time for a song request. Perhaps he knew a song I didn't, maybe some long-forgotten one.

Seeing me coming, the piano player took one last powerful drag from his cigarette, snuffed it out, and turned to face me. I asked if he might play some long-lost song. He explained to me that he didn't merely play long-lost songs. He played songs I would remember, to conjure something I had forgotten. I told him to let it rip.

In seconds, the piano player was playing away, as though he already had the song planned. Of course, it was a song I knew. Hadn't heard it in forever. My uncle played it by the riverside one summer sundown, years ago. I could see the current, clear as the piano in front of me. I sat by the riverside, line in the water, pole in my hand. My dad sat next to me, baiting his hook with worms from a coffee can. My uncle sat next to him, playing his banjo along with the piano player, swigging from a tall jar of dandelion wine. I watched the water and waited. The river surface was glowing from the reflections of the fireflies orbiting above it like little stars. It smelled alive with every sort of sea monster. I *so* wanted one for myself. Something's nibbling at dad's line. Something bites mine, and it's something massive. It's pulling on my pole with the force of a leviathan. I'm reeling. Dad's behind me, reeling with me. Uncle's smiling and strumming. I look beneath the water for my fish.

Instead of fish, I see herds of sunken spirits galloping with the undercurrent. I see Capricorn goats, sea horses, and selkies, all charging along the river bed. It's a kelpie on the end of my line. I could tell by the way it shape-shifted. One second it looked like a big old gator, slashing about, the next second a little water sprite, dancing about. I closed my eyes, pulling the pole with all my might. The harder I pulled, the harder I squeezed my eyes shut. The harder I squeezed my eyes closed, the stranger the memory became. The song rose

31

to a crescendo. The river overflowed. I was fully submerged. Every sort of sea creature swam by me, all around me, even straight through me. The water was iridescent, like splatters of every color paint on a shapeless canvas. Each bang of the piano keys brought forth a new burst of watercolors, and I was well in the past.

When the song finished, I was instantly returned to the present, to the Inn. Opening my eyes, I was surprised to see I'd been joined by a beautiful woman. She was seated next to me, smiling. I smiled back. I was sure I knew her from somewhere, but was too busy with other memories to consider hers any further. I was feeling deeply troubled at all I'd forgotten. Most of my life was already forgotten. I wondered at those many memories, so far gone, I couldn't even remember remembering them –all the sweets, stories, the summer nights. The woman smiled at me again, as if to say, "It's alright." Weird. The piano player laughed, as if he was in on it, whatever *it* was.

The woman gently touched my hand. My heart turned a somersault in my chest. I couldn't decide whether I was afraid of her, or the passage of time. I wondered at those memories lost, never to return. Try to remember, try to remember. What did you have for breakfast yesterday? Did you floss this morning? When was the last time you did this, or that? I tried to remember the first memory I'd had at the Inn. It was already hazy. I was almost panicking, desperately trying to remember, when the woman touched my face, steering it toward hers like a professional. Remember! Will you remember today? Will you remember tonight? Will you remember this strange little tavern of memories?

Then she kissed me, and I forgot it all...

A Strange Hangover

I woke up in my guest room with you guessed it - a strange hangover.

It wasn't that I was physically sick with your run-of-the-mill hangover symptoms. I wasn't even dehydrated. I was more disoriented, confused about the night before. The strangest thing about the hangover was the night before. It was like I'd blacked out, only I hadn't had a single drink. Had I? No. Yes. I had a memory, or two. I remembered remembering, but nothing after. I had no recollection of coming upstairs to my room from the bar. Someone, or someone's, had hauled me up to the room.

Speaking of the room, it was a nice little setup. Sleigh bed. Coffee table with coffee. Bathable bath. Fancy shampoo. Oil lantern. Oil painting of a cuckoo clock. No actual clock in the room, however. I could tell it was still morning from the pale shades of sunlight streaming in through the open window. Looking outside, I only then realized I was on the second floor. I stuck my head way out the window, breathing in that fresh, Nowheresville air.

Curious to solve the mystery of how I got upstairs to my

nice little room, I decided to go back downstairs to the bar, for answers. I'd find the bartender. He'd have answers. Bartenders have all the answers to all those profound questions of life, like how you got home last night.

I gave the horns a polish, dressed, and headed downstairs. Down in the bar, all was silent and still, that stale ale scent still lingering from the night before. The same faun bartender was behind the bar, looking like he'd never left. He was organizing, counting, cleaning, going through the mysterious morning motions of a bartender. Hearing me, he looked up, a smirk on his face. He was expecting me. Seemed he knew something I didn't.

"Morning mister. Early night last night..." His eyes were mostly down working as he talked, as if nothing out of the ordinary had happened to me, as if he'd had this conversation before, with hundreds of others he'd carried up or tossed out the night before.

"What happened to me?"

"What do you think happened to you?"

I had no idea.

"Poisoned, hallucinated, overserved. Maybe overserved on poisonous hallucinogens."

"Not exactly. I'd say you were more overwhelmed than overserved. As I said last night, The Forgetful Faun is no ordinary Inn. We serve only memories here. I am a brewer of the bygone, a doctor in days gone by, a priest of the past, and because all this town has is the past, our product is overflowing. Too much will put you squarely on your goblin ass, and if you have a low tolerance for nostalgia, you need be extra careful. You mister, have a low tolerance."

He served me a glass of water to drive that last point home, then pointed to a sign hanging from the bar. I hadn't noticed it the night before.

Warning

Spirits herein contain an infestation of every species of remembrance. Overconsumption may lead to time and spatial disorientation, as well as loss of consciousness.

"Well you don't say," was all I could think to say as I sipped my water trying to sort it all out. A few long minutes of awkward silence ensued, before the bartender noticed me not leaving.

"So, what brings you to the middle of nowhere?" he finally asked me.

"I grew up here, when it was still somewhere. I'm looking for someone, maybe you've seen her? She'd be a woman now. Name's Ruby Rockhollow. She used to live up on the north side of town. About yea high, face you'd remember. Used to be a big deal around here."

"Sorry, never heard of her. I'm not from the old days, I just serve em. When did you last see your Ruby?"

"Can't remember." I couldn't. There was no memorable

last goodbye for us. Just a slow, hardly noticeable, loss of touch over the years. That's how it always happens, so slow you hardly know to do anything about it.

"Do you remember when you first saw her? Maybe we start there, and work forward."

"When I first saw her? Must have been around the time she moved next door, maybe the first grade. Couldn't say when exactly. How am I supposed to remember that far back?"

"We're in the business of remembering, remember? I can whip up a little something fit for purpose, maybe a spirit to help conjure forgotten spirits, like this Ruby Rockhollow you're looking for. Shall I pour you a glass? Goes down like gravity. All you need is a sip."

"Fine." I trusted the bartender. He *had* carried me up to my room the night before.

The bartender went to work behind the bar, searching here and there for ingredients, mixing this and that. Clearly, it was no simple mixed drink, taking him all of a few minutes to prepare only a few ounces. The result was a sparkling, ruby colored concoction in a tulip glass, two maraschino cherries with a teeny cocktail sword through them.

"Voila!"

It tasted familiar, like a kiddie cocktail. Of course it did, because it probably was. I figured it was the bartender's idea of a joke. Taking a sip, I laughed like I was in on it. As it turned out, there was nothing to be in on. My eyes closed for me, as the enchanted cocktail remembered for me.

***

I'm six years old.

I'm a two, maybe three feet tall scraggly specimen, standing in the school gymnasium. My tiny heart is racing in my chest. I've been running, playing. I'm happy as ever, the happy only a little kid can be. I'm standing in the center of the gym, in a circle, among all the other kids in class. Within the circle is a rainbow-colored parachute. All us kids hold the parachute. I look around in astonishment at the familiar faces of old friends and classmates turned young again. The games begin before I find Ruby, but I know she's there.

We're playing parachute games. Maybe you remember these. A teacher throws some balls into the middle of the parachute. Popcorn! The kids all shake the parachute, laughing as the balls fly up and down and all around. We play merry-go-round, turning our little bodies sideways, holding the chute with one hand as we walk around in circles. We play see-saw, sitting down, pulling the parachute back and forth in see-saw motion.

We play fairyland.

In fairyland, teachers lift the parachute into the air, like a giant, colorful umbrella. Under the parachute is fairyland. All the kids run through fairyland, changing sides as quickly as possible, before the parachute falls back down on them. It's that long minute under the parachute in fairyland when teachers couldn't see that things got wild.

The gym teacher shouts "Fairyland!" as the parachute flies into the air.

I'm off to the races. Everyone is. Total anarchy ensues under the parachute. Little kids are running around, screaming, tackling, jump-kicking, cart-wheeling, laughing like lunatics. Caught up in the madness, I'd forgotten Ruby. I didn't see her at all before we collided. Our heads bounced off each other, then onto the floor, jolting stars above us, strange stars of fairyland.

I crawled over to her, holding my own aching head, to see if hers was alright. She was sitting cross-legged, in this cherry-dotted trapeze dress, crying softly into her hands. I felt like an evil villain for hurting her, but she looked ok, more scared than hurt. I sat down next to her. The parachute fell slowly down on us. With the other kids gone away, all was quiet in fairyland.

"I'm Ruby. What's your name?"

"I'm Icarus. I'm sorry..."

She smiled at me with a face wet with this tear / booger blend, taking my small hand in her even smaller one. The teachers were calling for us to come out from hiding.

"What do you want to be when you grow up?" She asked me.

"Dragon trainer." Obviously.

"When I grow up I'll be a princess, and live in a castle.

Will you visit me there?"

"Heck yes. I'll bring my dragon!"

"Yay!"

I lead her out of fairyland by the hand, back to the gymnasium, where we circled around the parachute again. She stood next to me, holding my hand a while longer when something strange happened. She stared at me, but she stared knowingly, as if she realized I was no boy at all, as if she knew it was only a distant memory. I stared back, trying to say something, anything, but the words wouldn't come. All I could do was stare at her. The memory was almost over. I could feel it ending.

She reached down, searching for something cleverly hidden in the hem of her dress. It was a tiny lighthouse trinket, like a Christmas tree ornament. She showed it to me, with this smile on her face, then slipped it into my pocket.

I looked curiously at her, just before the rainbow parachute faded to black.

***

I returned to consciousness as quickly as I'd lost it. I sat on the same barstool, the most potent kiddie cocktail in the history of kiddie cocktails in front of me. I hadn't even finished it. The bartender stood staring at me, polishing a glass, his face where Ruby's was, smiling, as she was.

"Well, go on. How was it? You weren't gone more than a few seconds."

I told him the story of the memory as you just read it. The bartender didn't say much, mostly nodding, head down, listening. He asked a few questions for clues as to Ruby's whereabouts, which I answered. We were having trouble finding any meaning whatsoever in the memory, when he asked me about the tiny lighthouse.

"The lighthouse. She put it in your pocket?"

"She did."

"Well, check your pocket."

Guess what was in my pocket?

Lighthouse of the Lost

There was the little lighthouse in my pocket, and according to my all-knowing bartender, another lighthouse, a full-sized one, just outside of town. No ocean for a million miles, but there was a lighthouse. God knew what purpose it served. Whispers around town spoke of a mysterious lighthouse keeper, one with magical powers. It was said he turned visitors into roosters and cast them from the top of the lighthouse. Sounded worth a visit. The bartender agreed to give me a ride out there later that same afternoon.

The lighthouse was further from town than I expected. From a distance, you'd have guessed it was no more than an old corn silo, and that would make sense because you'd be in farm country. But, if you looked closer, you'd see it was something else altogether, something not belonging to farm country. It was much too tall, and there was no farmhouse below it. There was something like a hat on the very top, and this speck up there, pacing the brim of the hat. It was no corn silo at all. It was the Lighthouse of the Lost.

The bartender pulled his pickup off the interstate onto a gravel road that ran toward the lighthouse. The road ran only a short while before dead ending at this impenetrable green wall of corn with stalks twice my height. He dropped me off there, wishing me well, promising a drink on him later when I returned to the tavern, *if* I returned to the tavern, muwhaha.

There was no path through the cornfield, so I made my way between the narrow cornrows, zig-zagging ever closer to the lighthouse. The tall stalks swayed and flapped noisily in the wind, sometimes bending and blocking my way. The lighthouse was tall enough for me to see, looming larger and larger, the closer I came. Eventually, I found a short grassy trail among the stalks, leading straight up to the lighthouse.

The lighthouse towered above me, seeming much higher than it had from the road. It was tree trunk shaped, thickest at the bottom, gradually narrowing on the way up. Built of massive, rough-cut granite blocks, the red front door looked bright, almost fluorescent against the gray rock all around it. There was a mailbox off to one side of the door, which struck me as odd. No chance anyone was delivering mail here, not through the cornfield.

There was no sign of anyone as I walked up. I lifted the brass knocker and dropped it lightly, which caused a thunderous explosion to reverberate through the lighthouse. I leapt back, wondering what in the hell had just happened. The whole structure quivered from the single knock, then quieted again. I waited a few unsure minutes, before daring to use the knocker again. After another, more delicate detonation, there was still no answer.

The door was unlocked, so I walked in.

Inside, I found the place soaking wet. Water was standing below, dripping from above, and flowing beside me, from the cracks in the walls. The air was salty, with hints of fishiness and seaweed. If I didn't know better, I'd have thought I was seaside. There was a spiral staircase leading up along the walls of the lighthouse, winding round and round, like some never-ending nautilus shell. Just staring at it made me dizzy.

"Helloooooooooo," I sounded the longest echo in history, up to the top of the lighthouse.

No answer.

I took a deep breath and started up the spiral staircase. There was no railing, so I walked slowly and carefully, keeping as near to the wet walls as possible. After spiraling up only a few stories, I started to feel queasy, not so much from the walking in circles, but from the wind outside, which was swaying the lighthouse. After a few more stories, I passed a little oval window, where I stopped for a rest and to peep out. I saw I was already higher than I'd expected.

As I climbed up, the spiral of the staircase began to shrink, the walls closing in on each side. When I was nearing the top I thought I heard footsteps from above. I looked up but saw no one. I was relieved when I did finally make it to the top, standing on a platform with a ladder leading up through a little round hole in the ceiling. Climbing up and through the hole, I found myself on a circular balcony with a panoramic view of the surrounding country.

Up there, high as I was, I imagined myself a goblin king. I looked down over my kingdom, across the endless countryside toward Rockville. I was captivated by the curious view, one without water anywhere in sight, yet the fields below resembled something like a body of water. Hills of cornfields rose and fell like swells in a golden ocean. Individual corn stalks swayed in the wind like whitecaps. Gusts blowing low through the fields made a ruffle like waves. I could see little red farmhouses peeking out of the fields here and there like scattered boats in the water.

I looked over my dominion, goblin emperor of the seven seas, when I got the idea/urge to take a piss right there off the lighthouse ledge. No one was around. Why not? Making sure the wind was at my back, I unzipped my pants and hung the most regal yellow line down unto my subjects. As I was doing so, I felt a tap on my shoulder.

I turned around in surprise, faced with what at first glance I thought was an ordinary man, with a full, bright orange beard. On second glance, I realized the orange was no beard at all, it was fluffy fur, and it covered the thing's face completely. The creature had the head of a house cat and the body of a human. It wore a long, navy blue sailor's pea coat and dark corduroy pants. Cat ears poked out of its woolen winter hat. A corncob pipe protruded through its whiskers. A spotted tail hung between two black fishing boots - two boots I'd just peed on.

Standing in front of me was what appeared to be a seafaring housecat.

"Welcome to the Lighthouse of the Lost, where the stars are strange and the buffalo range. I'm the lost cat, the lighthouse keeper. Are you yourself lost?" It sounded more man than cat.

"Hell... Hello, I mean..." was all I could muster, still stupefied, zipping up my pants as fast as I could manage. A handshake was out of the question.

"Well, what have you lost?" Pistachio cat eyes stared at me, unblinking.

"I, I have..." In my surprise, I'd forgotten what I'd lost.

"You have! If it's a thing you've lost, we almost certainly have it here. Here we have music videos, cursive, Atari, butterfly clips, Polaroids, polio, even Hooch. Did I mention paper maps? Sir, I have more paper maps than Christopher Columbus. No one needs maps anymore. They've all been lost. Lost maps of found places. Tell me, what is it exactly you've lost?"

"I've lost. Umm... Wait a second, what *have* I lost?" I thought aloud.

"You have lost a thought," the lighthouse keeper interrupted. "Is it a place you lost? We have mines, mills, malls, arcades, arcades in malls..."

"No, no, not a place. I remember now. I've lost a person."

46

"Of course you have, as has everyone. We have all sorts of lost persons here. We have cowboys, Indians, lamplighters, pinsetters, milkmen, miners... None of them? Let me guess, you're one of those who lost a girl? A princess? *The* princess?"

"Suppose I have lost someone along those lines. Ruby is her name."

"Ruby! Let's peek through the telescope, see if we can't find her."

The lighthouse keeper pulled a small device, rusted and worn, from his front coat pocket. If it was truly a telescope, it looked old enough for Galileo to have used. He pulled on one end, and the thing elongated, looking more like an admiral's spyglass than a telescope. Judging from its appearance, I didn't expect it to be so powerful. The lighthouse keeper handed it to me.

"That is a telescope unlike any in the world. That telescope is an optical instrument designed to rediscover all you've lost. It contains an arrangement of curved mirrors and memories, by which rays of forgotten light are collected and lost images magnified."

I brought the telescope to my eye, then to the sky. At first, I saw what I expected to see. The sun was sinking over the far horizon. Pinks and blues faded to purples and blacks. The stars flickered to life like faraway strands of fluorescent lights. It was only after the lighthouse keeper focused the lens that the view changed completely. Suddenly, I found myself looking at the night sky as I'd never seen it before, as a bizarre galaxy of the lost.

The first thing I noticed was a long-lost friend. The friend dangled from a star like a drunk from a chandelier, swinging and kicking his feet around crazily, looking straight down into my eyes, as if through the telescope itself. Next was a herd of ghosts, ghosting through the night like a pack of lost souls, darting here and there randomly. Across the face of the moon drove a lost memory. It was the old family station wagon putting by, my young-looking dad in the driver's seat, the boy Icarus Isakov sitting, smiling on his lap, doing the steering. I saw a grandmother clock, leaping from star to star - lost time. I saw lost boys, passing the second star on the right, going straight on until morning. The whole of space was crowded with the lost. My eyes dazzled with tears at lost words and ways, lost friends and family, at everything I'd lost. Everything that is, but Ruby. She was nowhere to be found.

"No lost princesses up there?" the lighthouse keeper guessed. "Can't say I'm surprised. Princesses, the lost ones, tend to stay lost either because they intended to, or were made to. I can help you find her, if you help me find something."

"What could I possibly help you find?"

"I've lost a letter, but no ordinary letter. I've lost a hand-written letter. A hand-written letter is far better than any typed letter because it holds meaning not just in the

48

words, but in the shapes of them. I've gleaned more from a single handwritten sentence than a thousand electronic ones. And if you must wait for a letter in the mail, all the better. Words age like whiskey. People have forgotten the thrill of opening the mailbox, and discovering a beautiful, suspenseful letter mixed among the bills and advertisements. Will you write me a letter?"

"That's it? All you want is a letter?"

"All anyone wants is a letter. Someday, when your adventure is over, I would like for you to write me a letter. It must be how a letter used to be. It must be handwritten. It must be long. It must be eloquent. It must be one of those sentimental letters, one you keep forever, like a book you never finished, or one you've read a hundred times."

"Fine."

"Fine? How will you write me a letter without knowing my address?"

The lighthouse keeper handed me a business card with his address. It read:

Lighthouse of the Lost
In a Sea of Corn Tossed
Adrift Down Main Street
Kissing in the Back Seat

"As for your lost princess, come we must commandeer the light of the lighthouse to find some sign of her."

The lighthouse keeper led me up a small staircase in the middle of the balcony to a tiny lantern room, where the navigating light was kept. I expected the light to be a huge, blazing globe of some sort, capable of illuminating the ends of the earth. How wrong I was. Inside the small room was a small desk. On that small desk stood a small lamp. The lamp looked like one of those antique banker's lamps, with a green shade and gold base, about a foot high. The lighthouse keeper tugged down on the golden cord, and the room turned emerald.

"Behold, the lighthouse light."

He must have read the disappointment in my face.

"I know, I know, not what you were expecting. I'll grant you, it is a modest navigational beacon, but I prefer it over a larger light. I find reading lights the most powerful lights of all."

The lighthouse keeper pulled a massive, medieval looking manuscript from a desk drawer and plopped it down with a thud.

"Behold, the lighthouse diary."

The lighthouse keeper blew a cloud of dust off, filling the room with that ripe, library book scent. He placed a monocle over one eye and began examining the giant diary silently. The cat-man lighthouse keeper, studying that ancient-looking manuscript, with his monocle, was a such a ridiculous sight it was all I could do not to laugh just looking at him. He flipped back and forth through the pages as if he were looking for some lost passage, but had no luck finding it.

"Would it help if I described to you what she looked like?" I asked.

"No, that would be of no help. Princesses are more common than you'd think. All girls are princesses, even if they live in tiny old attics, even if they aren't pretty, or smart, or young. Even so, they're still princesses. It is their right. An especially little princess once told me that."

After a little while longer, and making no apparent progress, the lighthouse keeper closed the manuscript, removed his monocle, and gazed up at me with those enormous, haunting cat eyes.

"I've had an epiphany."

The lighthouse keeper proceeded back down the stairs, out to a small ledge extending from the lighthouse balcony. I followed. We stood there, quietly looking out over the evening. The sky had darkened completely during the short period we'd spent in the lantern room. Lights from farmhouses flickered below like the stars above reflected in the sea. The wind strengthened. I could hear the swaying fields below like ocean waves. After a long minute, the lighthouse keeper spoke.

"Often, to find that which is lost, you must yourself get lost. Lucky for you, here at the Lighthouse of the Lost, we know of a way to get lost. There is a risk you'll never be found, but you may find what is lost. Shall we proceed?"

"How exactly will you get me lost? And where will I be?"

"If you knew where you were lost, you wouldn't be lost. Just look over there, above the far horizon line, at the stars shining closest to the earth, and imagine each its own setting sun."

I looked out, trying to distinguish the ground from the sky, when the lighthouse keeper moved behind me and whispered so closely in my ear, I could feel a jab from his whiskers.

"Remember to write me that letter."

The next sensation I felt was the lighthouse keeper's boot, kicking me squarely in my goblin ass. I went flying over the lighthouse balcony into the night, with hardly more than a gasp. I was too surprised to scream. I was plunging head first, straight down, toward certain death below. Looking down, trying to ascertain where exactly I might splatter, the dark fields appeared somehow different. The individual corn stalks joined together in a sea of green. I was confused and horrified for only a few seconds, until I splashed through what was no longer the corn field. Somehow it was now water.

I was lost at sea.

The Sea of Wishes

A brief recap of the story to now:

I received a distressing letter from the long-lost girl next door, so naively returned to my hometown to rescue the girl next door, where I found next door demolished, and the town mostly deserted, but did find an Inn, which served memories instead of drinks, where I had so many remembrances I couldn't remember, then had more memories, one of fairyland in gym class with the girl next door, who hinted I should visit a certain Lighthouse of the Lost, with a cat-sailor for a lighthouse keeper, who proceeded to ass-kick me from the very top of that lighthouse, into an ocean which appeared out of thin air.

Leading us to where we are now, with yours truly drowning.

Did I mention this was a strange story? Wait, it gets only stranger.

***

There I was, a sorry scrap of goblin debris, having just plummeted from the top of the lighthouse into the spontaneously appearing waters below. I was in a confused panic. Where did all this water come from? Why was I such an awful swimmer? Where would I swim, even if I could swim? I was struggling to even tread the choppy water. Just keeping my head above the waves took serious effort. To make things worse, the water smelled rank, like old well water.

A powerful current swept me away from the lighthouse. I didn't fight it. There was no point. What did it matter where I drowned? There was no land, no help, no anything, anywhere in sight. It wouldn't be long before I ran out of energy and sank to a watery goblin grave below. I tried to float on my back, to conserve energy. That proved only slightly easier than treading water.

After I'd drifted for what seemed like forever, my head floated into a rock. The rock was barely visible. I'd have passed it right by had I not accidentally bumped into it. It peaked out of the water like a turtle shell, just big enough for me to sit on. I used the last bit of energy I had to climb onto it, saved for the time being.

Looking around, I could tell I'd drifted far. The lighthouse was completely out of sight, and I could see the shadows of the mountains, nearer to town. I wondered if the town was also underwater.

THE IMAGINED HOMECOMING OF ICARUS ISAKOV

I sat there, perched on my lonely island like some marooned gargoyle statue. I was shivering and hopeless. The sea level was rising, quickly. There was no escape from Davy Jones's Locker. This was it. I imagined how my body would be found and how the whole matter would be reported to family and friends:

Former Rockville resident Icarus Isakov, son of the late Arthur and Gidget Isakov, drowned to death in an ocean or lake or something he never knew existed before he drowned to death in it. Poor Icarus was searching for a lost Ruby in a town with no rubies. He is survived by a modest retirement account, his apartment in the city, and all the sick days at the bank he never used. Rest in peace Icarus. He was always the nicest goblin, wasn't he? Oh yes, nicest goblin you ever knew. Absolute tragedy. Will take every bit of one, maybe two whole days to forget Icarus Isakov ever existed.

Then, when all seemed lost, out of the blue below me rose an unexpected savior, a mermaid. "Helloooooo," She splashed up and out of the water, startling me nearly back down into the water. I couldn't decide whether her "hellooooo" was seductive, sarcastic, or seductively sarcastic.

She smiled at me, like she liked goblins. I knew then I was dealing with a mermaid of rarified taste. Mermaids do their fair share of saving, but never of goblins. Princely castaways, yes. Peter Pans, yes. They'll even save fisherman. Goblins though? Most mermaids won't look twice at drowning goblins. Drowning goblins are wiggling whale turds to mermaids. Mermaids are not in the goblin-saving business, making me probably the only goblin in history to be saved by one.

She swam into my soon-to-be submerged personal space. She looked like the Starbucks mermaid, with her endless, pumpkin orange hair woven through a silver circlet. Her skin was as pale as it comes. Her eyes twinkled with curiosity at this out-of-his-element goblin. She was as surprised to see me as I was her.

"I'm a wish. Are you also a wish?"

"A wish? Me? No, no...I'm just a goblin, who wishes he were a wish, if all wishes swim as well as you. Can't say I ever knew a wish. Nice to meet you."

"You've never met a wish! Why, you're drowning in wishes, this very second."

"Is that so? I thought for certain I was drowning in water."

"All this wetness is more than water. This is an overflow of wishes from the old wishing well. Do you remember the well? Surely you wished upon it, long ago, when you were young, when wishes were fulfilled not by Amazon, but by shooting stars, dandelions, and wishing wells. It was somewhere out in the woods on the edge of town. It looked like a wishing well. It was stony, grimy, and ancient. The bottom was deeper than deep, somewhere near the center of the earth. It smelled like rotten eggs, and wishes. It smelled like it does now."

That would explain the smell.

"The well has been periodically overflowing with unclaimed wishes ever since the mine closed, and the town along with it. There are no wishers left in town to claim us. There are so many of us, we've run out of room in the old wishing well. Look below you, into the water. Look more closely, and you'll see all the wishes down there."

I looked. Sure enough, vaguely beneath the waves, I saw faintly glowing objects. From above, I'd have guessed they were shining schools of fish or fluorescent forests of seaweed. Some floated near the surface, making the water seem shallow. They were everywhere. The water heaved with wishes that were about to drown me. The water was up to my neck.

"Ahem. I seem to have a problem. Would you perhaps be able to swim me to town? The Forgetful Faun Inn?"

"I do happen to be swimming back that way, toward town, back down the wishing well. But, we must hurry. I expect the waters will recede soon. Wait here, I'll get you something to breathe."

She dove under water for a long minute, returning to the surface lugging this gargantuan, copper diving helmet. It looked about a thousand years old, maybe a wish from

Atlantis. She strapped the apparatus around my head and neck, pulling me under the waves, just before the waves would have pulled me under anyway. My mermaid hero led me by the hand, swimming faster than ever despite the dead-weight goblin she towed along.

I could see clearly under the water through the front glass of the old diving helmet. There was a wonderland of wishes in the waters below. We must have drifted through every single wish ever wished into that old wishing well. First, we passed through a whole armada of children's wishes. Kids wish more than anyone, making those waters the most crowded. Masses of toys of every shape, size, and design imaginable flitted by, everything from jack-in-the-boxes to Justice League action figures. We passed through whole schools of superheroes. It seemed every kid had wings, soaring here and there, smiling, because every kid wishes they could fly. Next, we passed through the realm of teenage wishes. That was basically an underwater orgy. There were waterproof bonfires on the seafloor, complete with music and dancing. I heard the distant chorus of wishes as we drifted by. Lastly, we passed through some adult wishes, but there weren't many of these. Those wishes were mostly of the material sort. Money swirled about everywhere, like gross clumps of seaweed. There were some new cars floating about, stray mansions here and there, nothing too interesting. I preferred my passage through the youngest of wishes. Those wishes were most interesting; I guess because kids wish mostly to wish, to dream anything might be real.

Eventually, the waters cleared of wishes. It was just the mermaid and I, swimming through a calm blue sea. Then a navy blue sea. Then a midnight blue sea. Eventually, it became so dark I lost all sense of space. I couldn't make out anything above or below me, or tell how deep we were. I tried to remain calm. I had no idea which direction we were going, but we'd been swimming for long enough that I figured we should be close to the town.

At some point, we must have turned sharply up toward the surface. The waters gradually brightened, allowing for me to see we were traveling up through a narrow crevice with rock walls on each side. We must have been incredibly deep because it took several minutes of swimming straight up to finally reach the surface. I wondered where in town we'd emerge from the water, from the wishes.

We surfaced in town, but not where I expected. We came up through the little stream that circled the Forgetful Faun. I'd guessed it was no more than a few feet deep when I'd first crossed it the night before. That deceptive stream, thin as a needle, must have been as deep as an ocean. My mermaid rescuer unsecured my breathing apparatus. I was saved.

"Here you are," she said it like it was no trouble at all.

"Thank you for saving me, for saving a goblin."

"Don't thank me. Thank whoever wished for you to be

saved."

She smooched me a fast one on the lips.

"Wish for me at the wishing well sometime, like you used to."

There was that twinkle in her eye again as she smiled and dove beneath the stream, splashing me with a last flip of her tail fin before she disappeared.

I turned from the stream and started toward the Inn. It must have been early in the morning. I could see the tavern downstairs was closed for the night. I was so exhausted I hardly made it upstairs to my room. Without bothering to dry off, I collapsed onto my bed, where I dreamed myself into a memory. I dreamed myself a kid again, not more than nine or ten years old. I found myself at the old town roller rink of all places, the Rockville Rollerway.

The Florence Nightingale Effect

Most of my class went to the Rollerway the first Tuesday night of every month. I didn't look forward to those nights, but I had to go. My mother forced me to, afraid I'd be thought a recluse if I didn't. Those nights at the rink were like miniature school dances, only on wheels. They were highly awkward for me. Normally, those nights at the rink were unmemorable. Not that night. That night was the only one I remember much of anything from.

For some reason, I was roller skating at the roller-skating rink that night. Me actually skating was rare, because I couldn't skate. I mean I really couldn't skate. I was a grave danger to myself and everyone around me when I put on roller skates. Ordinarily, I passed the hours at the rink with my shoes on, hanging out around the arcade, putting out the vibe, playing Galaga or Pac-Man. Lord knows how I ended up skating that night, but I did.

I rented a pair of those barf-colored disco skates with the bright orange wheels. They looked like the first model roller skates ever invented, and skated like it. The wheels hardly spun. The toe stops were worn down to nothing. The boots stunk of foot fungus. Oh well. I figured I'd only have the skates on a little while.

I skated, if you could call what I was doing skating. It was more a plod, or shuffle. I skated like that, careful to stay along the exterior of the rink, where there was a railing for me to hold onto. I was skating slower than I could walk. The rest of the skaters whizzed by me, some pointing, laughing. It was hard for me to pay them any attention. I was too busy clinging to the railing, just trying to survive another lap.

I did survive another lap, and a few more after that one. I was getting the hang of it, skating at a faster, more respectable speed, though still slow, still safely near the railing. After a while longer, I was feeling confident enough to skate on my own, away from the railing, closer to the center of the rink. I ventured out there, into the traffic, and couldn't believe it. I was smiling, skating, actually enjoying myself. Bubblegum rock blared, strobe lights blinked, and neon shadows danced on the hardwood beneath me. What mad genius invented the roller rink? Everything about the scene was suddenly exhilarating. I glided across the floor and felt like I was flying, like I was one of the cool kids.

What fun roller skating was!

I didn't see what happened next, though I heard plenty about it afterward. Apparently, as I was rounding a corner, and in an especially precarious position, a homicidal cyclops skated across the rink toward me at the speed of sound. I didn't see him, but I felt him. He cross-checked me, roller derby-style, into another dimension. I went flying, head over heels, smashing the back of my skull into the solid rink floor. I hit my head so hard that I saw stars. I saw them as only you can see them from a small town. There were whole galaxies in motion above me, as I lay there, half-conscious. The moon appeared, big and bright above me, laughing at me, like everyone else at the rink. The moon was so bright, I couldn't see much of anything else, so I shut my eyes.

When I opened them, Ruby's face was where the moon had been. I hadn't seen her skating before then, but she'd clearly seen me. She was looking down at me; this horrified look on her face, like the way you look down on a corpse at a wake. Others skated around her, looking down with that same look. Ruby helped me up, touching the knot on the back of my head. She and some others helped me off the rink. Someone got me an ice pack for my head. I sat down on a bench, humiliated, hating myself for ever having tried to skate in the first place.

As I beat myself up, the lights dimmed, and the music slowed. It was a couple's skate. Great. I always hated that part of the night. It seemed like every single kid found someone to skate with, everyone but me. Not that I expected anyone to ask me. You'd have to have a death-wish to skate with me. So, I was understandably surprised when Ruby grabbed me by the hand and forced me back out onto the rink. I told her no, that she was crazy, that I couldn't skate, that I'd kill us both, but she made me.

I skated forward as Ruby skated backward so that she was sort of towing me along. She was a much better backward skater than I was a forward skater, which meant I didn't have to skate much at all, thank God. That first lap, we held hands. The second lap, she moved in closer, putting my hands firmly on her hips. I wondered why she did that. Holding hands was one thing, but holding hips? I was still just a kid, after all. Ruby may have also been just a kid, but she was different. She always seemed years older than me. I think she would've kissed me then, if she thought I was ready for such a thing.

When the couple's skate ended, my head felt better. I felt better. Ruby had fixed me. She made sure to get me off the rink in one piece. I shuffled toward the skate rental. Time to go home.

"See ya at school Icarus."

"See ya Ruby."

I did see Ruby in school the next day. The cyclops who demolished me, on the other hand, I did not see in school the next day. He was absent. He was gone because he couldn't see.

Ruby punched his eye shut, later that same night.

A Curious Castle

I rose just before noon, damp and hungry. After washing myself of wishes, I hurried downstairs for something to eat. I was relieved to find lunch being served. My bartender was on duty. He was never off duty. During my whole stay there, I never saw another bartender. Didn't matter the day or time of day, he was a permanent fixture behind the bar.

I plopped my starving goblin self on a barstool. The bartender read my mind, delivering me the most ravishing cheeseburger and fries. I atomized every shred of food on the plate, then ordered some cheese fries to fill in the corners. I washed it all down with a venti fountain coke. Comfortably full, I felt healed from the long, surreal night before.

"Out late were we?" the bartender asked.

"Late enough to go scuba diving through a sea of wishes."

I told the story of my most peculiar mermaid adventure as you just read it, polishing off a picnic-sized basket of cheese fries in the process. The bartender went about his business behind the bar, shaking his head, sometimes pausing, asking for greater detail or clarification at this or that point in the story. He seemed surprisingly unsurprised at the whole matter. He was always like that.

"Ask me, sounds like one helluva night. I mean, mermaid rescuing a goblin from a cataclysmic flood of wishes? Strange. Too strange for coincidence. You say she introduced herself as a wish? I wonder if she wasn't more wish than she was mermaid. Might just be there is someone, somewhere, wishing mermaids into existence for the purpose of saving you."

"Doubtful." Because it was.

"What's on the agenda today?"

I had no plans for the day, or the rest of the week for that matter. I was still tired. After lunch, I planned to adjourn to my room, read a book, take a nap, and repeat that pleasant cycle until dinner. The bartender must have figured as much.

"Get outta here, go see what to see around town. There *are* things to see, if you know where to see them. Go have a drink with the old priest. Since the church closed, all he takes is red whiskey over on the corner of Main and Central. Old geezer sits there all day, every day, praying for a friend. Go ask him where your lost Ruby is. If anyone has any idea, it'd be him."

The old priest was none other than Priest O'Hagan. O'Hagan was an Irish elf, and that is not to be confused with a leprechaun. Irish elves may look like leprechauns, but they're something altogether different. Though well-liked by most in town, he was widely regarded as probably the worst Catholic priest in the whole history of Catholicism. He swore, drank all the communion wine, had affairs, and he gambled away tithes. He broke the nose of a Protestant minister from one town over for being the Protestant minister from one town over. One morning, when I was a kid, I found him passed out in the old church graveyard. After I shook him awake, he told me not to worry, because he'd be sure to confess his sins to himself in confession. When the mine closed, he declared himself an atheist, yet continued in the performance of his sermons and other priestly duties, right up until the church finally closed. How he was never defrocked, or excommunicated entirely, was always a great mystery.

I decided to pay him a visit.

***

I ventured out of the Inn only to be ambushed by a scalding afternoon. Scalding afternoons are more scalding for me than they are for you because your average goblin is borderline allergic to sunlight. We have some genetic aversion to it, maybe an inheritance from our distant ancestors who dwelt almost entirely underground. Anyway, the short walk from the Inn to downtown left me a sopping mess.

I found the old priest right where the bartender said I'd find him. He sat alone at a thankfully shaded table for two, outside an old, boarded-up café, which I thought unusual until I remembered the unusualness of O'Hagan. On the table sat a bottle of what turned out to be red whiskey, as expected. He saw me and waved me over excitedly.

"Virginless Mary! If it isn't Icarus Isakov!"

"Father."

O'Hagan was one of the strangest configurations of matter you ever laid eyes on. He looked like the love child of Abraham Lincoln and Elrond. He wore a dark, three-piece suit of suffocating wool, those pointy elf ears protruding from under a matching top hat. He was mostly bald, except for a few thin strands of peach fuzz on the back of his neck, his once legendary mullet clinging to life. His eyes still seemed to gleam with something young in them.

"Sit, *sit* my son. It's hotter than a whorehouse on nickel night. Here, have a glass of the sacrament."

I was steaming. If the table wasn't shaded, I'm sure I would have died of heatstroke right then and there. The old priest poured me a too tall glass of whiskey, then started talking. He loved to talk.

"Icarus my boy, you're aging like a piece of plastic. Not me. I'm old as Methuselah, and spoiling faster than a glass of milk. Still got it though. Guess what I was doing when you just walked up?"

"Sitting? Drinking? No. Sitting *and* drinking."

"I was meditating. Did you know that drinking whiskey is the most refined form of meditation for an Irish elf?

Meditation is the psychological process of bringing one's attention to the present moment. Nothing is better fit for such a purpose than whiskey. Tomorrow? Yesterday? After only a glass or two, those places become non-existent. Drink for long enough, and the concept of time disappears completely. Slightly drunk, I'm present as a cow in a pasture. Seriously drunk, I'm impossible to distinguish from the Buddha himself. Distilled alcohol is distilled magic, and pubs are sacred temples of time transcendence."

I took a sip from the whiskey he gave me. The taste was not exactly transcendent.

"Do you know why there is always that mirror behind a bar?"

"No." I never wondered at the ever-present bar mirror.

"That mirror is used for meditative purposes. You can't be anywhere but here and now when you see your own reflection in a bar mirror. There is no past or future in a bar mirror, only that very second. The bar mirror presents a portrait of the present, forever and ever.

I thought about the mirror behind the bar at the Inn. That was no ordinary mirror. It was a funhouse mirror. It made the reflection younger. It presented the past, not the present.

"Tell me, what brings a big-time, city-goin' goblin like yourself back to this one-horse, horseshit-pile of a hamlet? Didn't you know they closed the mine?"

"I heard, but I'm looking for someone. Do you

remember Ruby Rockhollow?"

"Oh of course, of course. Who could forget Ruby Rockhollow? I think she may be the only reason I remember you, no offense. You lived next door to her, if I remember rightly."

"I did."

"May I ask what is the exact nature of your interest in the girl next door?"

"Oh, purely platonic father." For a second, I felt like I was back in confession.

"Boys next door do not have purely platonic interests in girls next door."

"Is that so? Have you seen her around town lately?"

"I have not. I think no one will have seen Ruby for some time. She is one of those missing persons you never noticed went missing in the first place. She faded away gradually, after the old mine closed. You saw less and less of her around town, but because you saw less and less of everyone around town, you never noticed when she disappeared completely."

He downed the remainder of his glass, quickly pouring himself another. I wondered if it had any effect at all on him. He seemed as sober as a priest; a normal priest that is.

"Now, there were plenty of Rubies who disappeared, totally unaccounted for. Question is, where did they disappear to? Yes, many left when the mine closed, but others just poof, up and vanished like witch tits in the night. Where did they all go? Where, whe..."

70

The priest ran out of breath and, for half a second, I thought he was going to die right then and there on me. Then he closed his eyes and started deep breathing. He looked like he might really be meditating. He breathed like that for about a minute, then opened his eyes again. "Where was I? Ah, yes, the whereabouts of the disappeared. Allow me to hypothesize on that matter."

"After the mine closed, a most mystifying and wicked castle appeared. It sprung up like a giant, poisonous, mushroom in the middle of the night over across town, nestled right into the base of the mountain. No one saw it built, or knows who built it. No one knows who lives there, but they certainly live there. You can see them, only in the middle of the night, faceless phantoms and strange silhouettes lurking in the windows. No one leaves the castle, and no one is allowed in. There is a giant sonuvabitch gatekeeper draped in black armor, looks like a walking nightmare. They say the gatekeeper is the dreaded Watchman, the one from the old tales. That castle is a whole infestation of nightmares. I'm certain of it."

I knew of the castle. I'd noticed it when I first arrived in town and thought it bizarre then. The Watchman I hadn't noticed. The Watchman was a mythological manner of monster, alleged to roam the wilderness around town, occasionally wandering into town to terrorize the locals. I saw him only once, when I was a kid. More on him later.

"What makes you so sure the castle is evil?"

"I'm an ordained agent of the almighty, for Jesus Harold Christ's sake. I've been thoroughly trained in the identification of devilish castles. If you don't believe me, go have a look for yourself. The castle overlooks the town, exercising some sorcerous power over the people. It's not a power you can see, but you can feel it. The castle has somehow gained control over all the hopes, dreams, and imaginations of the inhabitants. Something from that castle is quietly kidnapping our spirits, one by one, like a thief in the night. I can't prove it, but I think the castle has something to do with the disappearances of residents, like your 'purely platonic' pal, Ruby. If you're looking for her, I suggest you go there."

politely forced the remnants of my whiskey down and thanked the priest. I planned on setting out toward the opposite end of town to see what there was to see with the castle. Before I left, the priest gave me an unusual blessing.

May the road rise up to meet you
May the hollow Hydra not fill up on you
May the wind be always at your back
May the Watchman have a heart attack
And until we meet again,
May God hold you in the palm of His hand
And pour me a stiff one with His other hand

I set forth toward the castle, determined to find Ruby.

THE IMAGINED HOMECOMING OF ICARUS ISAKOV

***

I made it less than half way to the castle.

The sun convinced me to turn around. The temperature was nearing natural disaster levels. I swear I nearly melted to death on the short walk back to the Inn. My body was on fire, head to toe. The soles of my feet sizzled with every step. My arms were blackened, dangling like licorice from my sides. My back had run out of sweat to cool it. My head was dizzy, my tongue begging for me to stop, for water. I needed water. I've never been so thirsty.

Somehow, I did finally make it back to the Inn. I hobbled, back bent like an old goblin, up to the front door, and couldn't have hobbled any further if the fate of the universe depended on it. Climbing the hill to the Inn felt like climbing Mount Everest. Inside, my eyes widened at a tin bucket of rainbow colors shining on the bar. In the bucket were precious green, blue, and red trophies – soda bottles. I chose a red soda, because red is the best soda. The label on the bottle read "Pioneer Strawberry Soda," and had this scribble of an old horse-drawn carriage, set against some snow-capped mountains, as though pioneers drank Pioneer Strawberry Soda.

I sat down rubbing the cold, sweaty bottle on my hot, sweaty neck. I wouldn't have traded that strawberry soda for its weight in diamonds. It tasted sweeter than anything in the whole wide world. After the first sip, I instantly felt cooled and cured, as if the soda itself had magical healing properties. I drank and drank, imagining the rich redness was blood, and I a vampire, fresh from the coffin, feeding to nourish my undead flesh.

Down the bar from me I noticed the drunken grandfather clock from the first night I'd arrived. He looked calmed down, sipping from a wine glass, reading the newspaper. I walked over to ask him the time. He was the only clock in the bar, after all.

"Excuse me sir, do you have the time."

The clock looked up from his newspaper.

"Yes." The clock looked down at his newspaper.

"Well, can I have it? The time?"

He looked up again. "You can't have time. It can have you, but you can't have it."

"I... I meant to say what time *is* it?"

"It is imagined. You are one of those who has mistaken imaginary for real. Flowers, foxes, lakes, lemons. Those are real. Laws, limited liability corporations, liberalism, conservativism, conservative liberalism. Those are imagined. Maybe commonly imagined, but imagined all the same. Time is the most imagined thing of all. Clearly, you have been bamboozled by time. The past never is. The future never was. The present I'll grant you, but hardly. No one notices it. No one notices the second hand tick on a clock. People only look at the minute and hour hand. Isn't that funny? The second hand is all that really matters."

He picked his newspaper back up, signaling an end to

the conversation. I'd finished my soda, and was feeling cooler, but not cool enough. The bar was all humid and sticky. I sought my bartender for a memory of snow. Snow would cool the day right down.

"Snow, in summertime? Crazy! So crazy, it just might work."

The bartender searched the bar top to bottom for my order of snow. He looked where I expected, in the fridge, but found nothing there. He was under the bar awhile but came up empty. He searched around the bottles behind the bar, no luck. Just when I'd begun to lose all hope, he reached up, his hand searching above an overhead glass rack, and found what he'd been looking for. It was a seemingly ordinary snow globe, which I, by this point, knew would be extraordinary. He handed it to me.

"Go on. Shake it."

As soon as I did, the bar miraculously cooled. I could see my breath. Frost gathered on the window panes. Icicles formed on the chandelier. Then came the snowflakes. There were only a few flurries here and there, until I took it upon myself to shake the snow globe again, harder. The wind blew up a wintry gale from nowhere, causing a full-scale blizzard. The bar itself looked like a freshly shaken snow globe, like an ice palace. It was freezing. The soda bottles froze. The bar taps froze. The grandfather clock stood there, still as ice, covered in frost. Time was frozen.

"Thank you," I laughed to the bartender. He smiled.

I closed my eyes, tilted my head back, opened my mouth, and caught snowflakes on my tongue. I recognized their taste. They tasted as they once had, once upon a time, in a land far, far away.

Where Snow Angels Go

When I was a kid, it snowed inside our house.

Snowflakes snuck in like tiny, burglarizing Santa's through our crownless chimney top, falling all the way down the flue, swirling into the fireplace, finally settling on the hearth in a watery mass grave. Drove mom crazy that dad never got around to crowning that chimney top. I think he secretly liked the snow. So did I. Every little kid loves snow, especially that first one of the winter season.

I was around ten years old. It was an early November day, normally too early for any serious snow. I remember being surprised by the sight of it, pouring in through our fireplace. I rushed to the window where I stared, hypnotized by the big white flakes weighing down the trees limbs, which were still bright with autumn color. Although it was snowing, the combination of whites, reds, and oranges looked to me as bright as any summer day.

Outside, kids were everywhere, each celebrating the unexpected snowfall in their own way. Snowmen were born, swords were forged from icicles, sleds raced through white drifts. After I'd shoveled the front walkway, I knocked on Ruby's front door. She opened it with a screaming bull charge, tackling me clear off the porch into a mound of snow. We shook the white off and set forth in search of some wintry adventure.

We trudged through the fast-piling snow toward a wide-open field in the center of the neighborhood where a battle was being waged - one so great, we could hear the screaming from blocks away. When we arrived, we came upon the largest, most epic snowball fight in the history of snowball fights. This was the Gettysburg of snowball fights. Hundreds of kids, creatures, spirits, monsters, and anything else you can imagine ran helter-skelter through the blizzard, throwing snow at one another in a maelstrom of white. There was a yeti hurling snowballs the size of watermelons. A team of some dozen dwarves lofted even larger snowballs back with a snow-catapult. An abominable-looking snowman wrestled a pack of dire wolves. Whelps dropped frosty projectiles from above. Snow came up from the ground, down from the sky, and in from every side.

We hurried into the fight, joining one of the two lines of opposing armies stretched out and facing one another, each behind its network of forts, walls, and trenches. There was a no man's land between the two lines, dotted with casualties. We joined up with a few classmates behind a short ice wall, where we had our first taste of battle, and it was magnificent. That early winter snow, moist and heavy, *was perfect for packing. We started whipping dense, white fastballs in the general direction of the yeti, who at around ten feet tall and half that wide, was the easiest of targets.*

I got off only a few good balls before taking a direct hit to the ribs. We'd been outflanked and surprised by a band of insidious trolls. They devastated us, hitting us with everything they had, including dozens of dreaded piss-yellow snowballs. Our side scattered in terror. Those who couldn't get away were whitewashed, or yellow-washed. No quarter was given. I'd have been an early casualty, had Ruby not dragged my wounded body into a nearby igloo for shelter.

Inside the igloo, we were surprised by the sight of twenty or so gnomes, sitting cross-legged along the walls, the unmistakable scent of hot cocoa rising from the tiny thimbles they sipped. We were not offered any. Sensing we were not welcome, we scrambled back outside, and only just in time. Just a few feet away, we saw an ice dragon swoop down and decapitate a giant-sized snowman. The dragon flew above us like a B-29 bomber, dropping the huge head onto the igloo roof, where it crashed through with a white explosion, leveling the whole place. Grumpy, shell-shocked gnomes dug themselves out in a mess of hot chocolate and frost, looking like little snow-covered turds.

We returned to the front lines, where our side had reformed after successfully defending from the troll onslaught. The fight raged on for untold hours, each side barraging the other with an endless arsenal, constantly resupplied, one flake at a time, from the invisible arms dealer above. I chucked snowball after snowball, inflicting casualty after casualty, until I'd thrown my arm out entirely, then kept chucking. Ruby was by my side the whole time, massacring countless enemy along with me, watching my six for yellow-snow lobbing trolls.

Finally, when the white sky turned gray, my socks turned a frosty blue, and my face turned a soon-to-be frostbit scarlet, I decided to get myself dramatically killed. I thought a dramatic death would impress Ruby, and anyway I wanted to go home. I leapt over a snow-wall into no man's land with a rebel yell, charging in a berserk battle frenzy toward the enemy lines. It was a glorious sight for the five seconds it lasted and I was riddled with a volley of what felt like hundreds of snowballs. I tumbled headfirst into the snow, to gasps and cheers from all.

Laying in the snow, blood trickling from my nose, I gave up the ghost. She was a snow angel. I made her right there in the cold below me under the whizz of snowballs. As soon as I'd finished, I saw her, this white-robed, straw-haired little girl with glimmering wings of ice, floating up into the blizzard. She looked like the Ghost of Christmas Past. As she rose to life, the battle fell silent, everyone staring at her, stupefied. I waved to her. She waved back with this slow, half-smile. She didn't stay long, soaring higher and higher up into the gloom, finally blending in *with the snowflakes, going wherever snow angels go.*

I crawled out of no man's land back toward my own line. Ruby was waiting for me. She looked impressed. Mission accomplished. She wiped the blood from my nose with her hat and gave me a nod toward home. War-weary, we started the walk back together, arm in arm, into the teeth of the wind. It was no easy march for a goblin casualty like me, but I didn't let on how hard it was.

By the time we finally made it home, my mouth was so numb with cold, I could hardly say goodbye.

"Thee ya later alligator."

"After while crocodile."

I found it no longer snowing inside my house. A hulking log blazed in the fireplace, melting the flakes before they could sneak inside. I collapsed onto the couch, reimagining scenes from the day's battle within the fire. Staring tiredly into it, I saw smoldering snowballs, fire-breathing ice dragons, mutilated and melting snowmen, red wolves howling over the crackling of the fireplace, and of course Ruby, dancing among the flaming mayhem. I looked outside, where the storm raged on. Eyelids heavy, I managed one last glance out the window, up into the silvery sky, looking hopelessly for some sign of my snow angel, before closing my eyes.

The Mine of Secrets

Back at the Inn, the snow stopped quick as it started. After an early dinner, I called it a night. I needed the rest. I planned on an expedition to the curious castle the next morning. I hoped for some sign of Ruby there, though wasn't exactly sure how I'd get inside. The priest said the castle was inaccessible, guarded by the dreaded Watchman. I figured I'd find a back door, or scale the outer walls, or something. The bartender had other ideas, stopping me on my way out that next morning.

"Frosty the goblin-man, where you off to in such a rush?"

"Sightseeing at the castle for a certain Ruby."

"*The* castle? Buster, you're wasting your time headed there. I hear no one's allowed in, or out for that matter. Word around town is the one-and-only Watchman guards the front door. Let me save you the trip and tell you how your trip will go. You'll go to the castle, where you'll encounter the Watchman. If you're brave enough to ask him to let you in, he won't let you. He may just murder you and make himself a light snack of your brains."

"Well then, how am I supposed to get inside the castle?"

"Don't know, and even if I did, not sure I'd go, or advise in your going there. Have you *seen* the castle? It looks like Castle Dracula. I'm perfectly happy here behind the bar, robbing the present from you with the past, thank you very much."

The bartender served me a Mexican Coffee, then went missing in the kitchen. I sat around the Inn awhile, sulking. The coffee, though delicious, was of no help. Mexican Coffee is more of a depressant than a stimulant. The thing about depressants is, they mostly make you more depressed. The trip so far had been a magical mystery tour to nothing. No one had seen Ruby in eons. What chance did I have of finding her? I'd already nearly drowned to death and been melted alive. Maybe it was time to cut my losses, arrange for transportation back to the city, back to my apartment, back to work and normalcy. Back to the present.

As I finished my drink, the bartender returned from the kitchen. He stood in front of me, polishing his horns uneasily with a bar rag. He wanted to help me, just didn't know how.

"Listen, if you're hell-bent on going to the castle, you'll need to find some secret, maybe a secret way in, a secret password, or some other secret something. This town has secrets everywhere if you know where to find them. I hear there is a concentration of secrets, among other things, down in the old abandoned mine."

"I thought the mine had already been mined?"

"Mined of rubies, yes. But, they say there are plenty of other curiosities down there. They say there are mazes and monsters down there. They say spirits sing and dance down there. They say there are secrets down there, and who knows, maybe a secret just for you..."

***

The old mine wasn't a far walk. Nowadays, it's hardly noticeable, out in the middle of a field overgrown with poppies on the outskirts of town. From a distance I could see it, rising like a gingerbread house from a sea of red gumdrops. Up close, its color changed from gingerbread to this black-brown, decayed color, and I could see just how abandoned it really was. The mine was now a pile of rotted timber in the shape of a barn.

For me, the forsaken mine was a sad sight. My old man spent half his life in that mine. He'd grown old before his time down there, working his skin from amber to ash, curving his back crooked as the winding trail that led there, now buried in weeds. I wondered what dad would've thought of the remnants. Probably better he wasn't alive to see them.

I walked cautiously through the front door of the pile. Inside, there was little to see but dusty, collapsed wooden beams all around, and a dark passageway in one corner. That dark passageway was the entrance to the last accessible mine shaft. A sign stood outside it with an arrow pointing in, reading:

Danger

Secret Excavation of Secrets in Progress

I wondered if a secret excavation of secrets was still secret if a sign announced it. A small lantern sat below the sign, as if someone was expecting me. I picked it up and started through the shaft. The tunnel was an ordinary looking one, with Y shaped wooden pillars holding up the ceiling and straight wooden planks nailed against either side of the wall. Unlit lanterns dangled above from a cold draft. The shaft had hardly any collapsed beams, making it seem strangely maintained, unlike the rest of the mine.

The path sloped steadily downward a while, before opening into a larger space. Once my eyes adjusted to the darkness, I found myself in a vast cavern. The ceiling was high and decorated with shining stalactites hanging there like miniature upside down kingdoms. At the far corner of the cave was a little glow. The glow shone from the little headlamp of a dwarf. Here was what I assumed correctly to be a secret miner, mining for secrets. I could hear him huffing and puffing, swing his pickaxe into the same boulder, over and over. Looked exhausting.

"Ahem," I ahemmed.

The lone miner spun around, standing perfectly still a moment, staring across the cave at me a few seconds, before resting his pickaxe on his shoulder and strolling forward. He was as dark as the mine. He wore black overalls that matched his long black beard, which hung nearly all the way to the ground. His face was so black under his black helmet, you couldn't tell where the darkness of the mine stopped and his skin began. The white of his eyes whirled and blinked like fireflies in the night as he came closer.

"Hello there. I'm Icarus Isakov. May I ask what it is you are mining for?"

"Hullo, Last Miner at yer service. As for what I'm mining fer, you done not read the sign. I'm fixin to quarry secrets from these here rocks. Not just any ole secrets. I'm mining fer the deepest, darkest of secrets. This town is chock full-a em, let me tell ya."

He put down his pickaxe and walked closer to me, sizing me up, before continuing.

"I reckon them most interesting secrets is all them that was kept from ya. The girl who secretly wanted to kiss ya. The girl who secretly kissed someone else. The friend who always wanted to be ya. And the one who despised ya. The secrets your pa never told ya, because he couldn't. The secrets your ma never told ya, because she wouldn't. All those secrets is here, if ya mine deep enough. Tell me, is there a secret yer looking fer?"

"No," I responded, quickly and nervously. The miner asked the last question as if he personally owned all the secrets in the mine. I didn't want to offend, by staking my own claim.

"Come now, nothing to be afeared of, there's plenty of

secrets down here."

"Well, now that you mention it, there is a secret I could benefit from learning. It's the secret to the castle I'm needing to get my hands on."

His eyes widened at my mention of the castle.

"I see you is a bold goblin then. That perticular secret would be somewhere deep and dark indeed. It wouldn't be in this here cavern. In here is all little white lies. I'm digging up ole girlfriends in here like a gawd dang lunatic."

The dwarf took off his helmet. His hair was long, greasy and black as the rest of him. He stood on his tippy toes, gazing into my eyes.

"Cumear, I have a mine car git us straight over to a cavern that may or may not contain yer secret."

The dwarf turned his headlamp back on and signaled for me to follow him. We walked to the far end of the cave, into a narrow shaft. In there, sat a single rusty minecart on some even rustier tracks, which traveled downward into the dark, unknown depths of the mine. We hopped into the cart, myself in front, my dwarf guide snugly behind. He insisted I sit in front because, "It'd be a lick more fun that way."

The minecart started down quickly at first, then more slowly as the slope lessened. The cart rode clumsily on the rails, trembling as it rolled forward. I trembled with it. A single dim light shone from the front of the cart, shedding light only a little ahead and less to each side. For the first part of the ride, we rolled quietly onward, with little to see but the darkness ahead.

After a few minutes, I smelled an unexpected smell. The scent of raspberries and strawberries replaced the funk of dirt and dust. The mine wall on our left disappeared, opening on to a dark river running parallel to the track. The river flowed swiftly enough for me to hear it over the clankity clank of the cart wheels. It looked dark and dangerous, yet smelled strangely sweet.

"The deeper you delve here, the more secrets you tend to discover. Take that there river. That ain't water. That's a fine wine. That river flows with all the deep secrets that come from a fine wine. The later in the night it gets, the higher the river flows, because most of them secrets is revealed late at night, after indulging a glass or three."

I peeked over the side of the cart into the river. Sure enough, it looked like wine. I wanted to dive in, but soon the red river veered away, and the mine wall returned. We continued in our zig zagging through the darkness, until the opposite wall flattened completely. Doors started appearing in the wall, a new one every few seconds. The doors were all shapes, sizes, and colors. They looked harmless enough, yet something about them worried me.

"Where do these doors lead?"

"Shhhh! Yappin be damned! Ya talk too loud, and they'll awaken. In them doors is nowhere you'd hope to go."

"Awaken who?" I whispered. "What's inside all those doors?"

THE IMAGINED HOMECOMING OF ICARUS ISAKOV

"Them is closets. In them closets is skeletons. Don't want to wake them. There's hazardous secrets in closets. And once skeletons leave the closet, they aren't apt to return."

The cart rolled on slower than ever, to my annoyance and fright. Every time it rattled a little too loud on the tracks, my heart rattled with it. I started to feel claustrophobic, but there was nothing I could do, nowhere I could go. Getting out of the mine cart was out of the question. All I could do was stare unblinkingly at the strange rows of closet doors, skeletons lurking within.

After a little while, the closet doors appeared less and less often. I was hopeful we'd soon be out of harm's way when a treacherous, cupcake-sized boulder appeared on the track ahead. I knew it was trouble, because of it how it sat, so perfectly on the rail like it was intentionally placed there by some secret saboteur. I watched helplessly as the cart rolled toward it. When we hit it, the rock split open with a crack like thunder that echoed endlessly through both ends of the cave. Not a second after, a parade of skeletons burst through the closet doors, swarming crazily at us from behind.

The miner threw his pickaxe like a tomahawk in the general direction of the skeletons chasing us. It crashed into them with a glass-shattering sound, but did little to slow their attack. Swarms of skeletons flooded from the closets, running faster than ever after the cart. One skeleton made it in the cart, but lost his head when it collided with a low-hanging stalactite. Never, ever stand up in a moving mine cart. When the rest of the skeletons were only a few feet behind us, the tracks turned sharply downward, helping us gain some speed and separation. A few unlucky skeletons came out of their closets in front of us as we sped downward. We smashed clean through them, sending bones flying in all directions.

As we sped away, the tracks started to meander crazily. The minecart was like an out of control rollercoaster. We were twisting, turning, and barrel-rolling forward at an incredible speed. I can't explain how I didn't fly out of the cart and die a grisly death, but I didn't. Eventually, the tracks straightened out, but the cart didn't slow. It went faster and faster, as if powered by some invisible engine. Finally, when it seemed the cart couldn't possibly go any faster, we exploded through the thin curtain of a waterfall into a dark cavern.

I leapt out the second we stopped, vowing never to ride a minecart again. The miner spat on the ground, looking unfazed. He turned his headlamp on and signaled me to follow him.

"We're deeper than the nethermost pits of hell, so stay nigh."

I took his advice as we ventured into the darkness. The ceiling of the cavern was so high and dark I couldn't see it at all. If I wasn't so far underground, I might've mistaken it for a starless sky. There wasn't much below, either. It was just the miner and me, and the bit of shine from his helmet lighting our way.

We came upon a narrow tunnel, leading toward a dim, orange glow at the far end. The glow was from candles lighting a most unusual room, not the sort you'd expect to find in the depths of an abandoned mine. The room was finished, for one thing. It had stone floors, painted walls, and an arched ceiling of big timber beams. A dragon-tooth chandelier dangled overhead. There were keys everywhere. There were paintings of keys, sculptures of keys, and actual keys. There was even a Keystone beer. A street sign read "Open Sesame" on the far wall, above a bookshelf with the most colorful, curious-looking books. On one of the shelves, a goldfish swimming in a waterless bowl acted as a bookend. I felt like I was in Willie Wonka's private study.

"Welcome one and all to the hall of secret keys and passwords and strangeness. Ya best start looking fer what yer looking fer."

The bookshelf seemed a good place to start in my search for the secret to the castle. I'm drawn to bookshelves like a zombie to human flesh. Been that way since before I could even read. The bookshelf held no ordinary collection of books. It was filled with secret publications. There was *Jay Gatsby's Champagne Cellar of Speakeasy Passwords*, *The Independent's Guide to Secret Fraternal Handshakes*, *Freemasonry for Dummies: Secrets, Signs, and Grips*, and more like that.

I found myself flipping through *The Secret to Everlasting Life*, when the miner interrupted me.

"Reckon I found something intended fer ya."

The miner handed me a present no bigger than a shoebox. It was wrapped in this circus-looking wrapping paper, making it look like a big box of animal cookies or a child's birthday present. My full name was scribbled in black marker on the top.

"Found it sittin' in the corner, like someone knew we was coming."

I tore off the wrapping paper. Inside was a box. Inside the box was a dreamcatcher, and not just any dreamcatcher. It was my old dreamcatcher, the very same one that hung over my bed when I was a kid. I hadn't seen it in years but could tell straight away it was mine. It didn't look like any old dreamcatcher. Your standard dreamcatcher has a willow hoop, with a net-like a spider web wove over it. It might also have some peacock feathers or rabbit's feet dangling from it, because why the hell not. My dreamcatcher was different. It had a Ferris wheel instead of a willow hoop, and spokes of the Ferris wheel instead of a spider web. Dangling from the Ferris wheel was a fluffy purple monkey, a sack of marbles, a little toy robot, and a few other carnival trinkets. I was happy to be reunited with it, but it wasn't the sort of secret I was expecting. I wondered what it had to do with Ruby, and the castle.

"This is it? My dreamcatcher? What exactly am I

supposed to do with it?"

"If secrets was obvious, they wouldn't be secrets at all. Trust me, that there trinket will serve its purpose, else it wouldn't be all this way down here."

Needless to say, I was flustered. It seemed to me there was a new secret, the one to the dreamcatcher, that needed solving. Sounded like a suitable riddle for the bartender.

The trip out of the cave was a long one. At first, the miner suggested we ride another minecart, up and out this time, instead of down and in. I respectfully refused the offer. We'd walk up and out. It took longer, but was undoubtedly safer. I followed the miner through a network of tunnels so dark, twisting, and turning that at times I wondered if we weren't lost. It seemed like we walked for hours, but it couldn't have been that long. The sun was only just setting when we emerged from the underground. I was dead-tired.

Before we parted, I asked the miner a question I'd been meaning to ask.

"What secret are you mining for?"

"That's a secret."

He disappeared with a chuckle into the mine.

***

The Inn was busy that night. There was a band of gypsies belonging to some long-lost race of moon elves passing through town. I could tell they were moon elves from all the star-dotted caravans, astrological cloaks and what not. A dozen or so wagons surrounded the base of the hill like they were besieging the Inn. They turned out to be nice enough, mostly sitting around the fire, drinking, telling stories. I was at a nearby table, finishing dinner when one of them motioned for me to join them.

They were telling ghost stories from all those faraway lands they'd visited. They told tales of banshee wails heralding the death of kings, and their roaming ghosts haunting barren castles. They described devourers of the dead, soul swallowers, headless horseman, ladies in white, ladies in red, and every sort of ghost you could imagine. There were ghost ships haunting the high seas, vanishing hitchhikers vanishing in the back seat, murdered peddlers selling housewares, and plenty more along those lines.

The gypsies asked me for a ghost story, one from Rockville. They said there must be ghosts practically falling from the sky in a town like this. Where did they live? In the graveyard by the woods? In the river in the woods? In the mountains over the woods? They all eventually agreed the local ghosts most likely lived in the castle nearest the mountains. The castle looked about as haunted as Halloween. Surely, there must be ghosts within the castle.

"Go on Icarus, tell us of the ghosts of Rockville," they pleaded. "Tell us of the ghosts in the castle."

I did, but there was only one ghost in town to tell of.

The Watchman

Every small town has a mysterious, mythological monster. You know the type. Pennywise. Karl the Giant. Freddy Krueger. Pap Finn. The thing from Stranger Things. Well, ours was the Watchman.

Plenty was said about the Watchman. It was said he lived in the deepest, darkest woods up on the mountainside at the far end of town. He only came out at night. He wore a cloak of night, making him almost indistinguishable from the night. It was said he'd creep into town. That he'd steal babies from their cribs, devour puppies, torture kittens, murder the occasional grandmother, and so on. That's what was said, anyway.

The truth was, no one knew who the Watchman was. That didn't stop everyone from pretending to know. There were endless theories. Some claimed he was the last ancestor of an ancient race of mountain trolls. Others claimed he was an abandoned ogre child who'd been raised by wargs and wolves. Some said he was Bigfoot. My dad said he was no more than a goblin gone crazy. My mom said he was no more than a figment of the town's imagination.

Grandpa loved to rant about the Watchman. Gramps said the Watchman was once a great goblin knight. He'd left his family in town to fight in the great goblin wars. While away, he was reported to have been killed in action. Assuming him dead, his family left town, off to who knows where[3]. Turned out, the great goblin knight wasn't killed at all. He was only taken prisoner. Once released, he returned to town with a crippling case of PTSD and an empty home, both of which drove him crazy. He's been crazily roaming the wilderness around town ever since, waiting, watching for his family, living on a strict diet of townsfolk flesh.

Growing up, whatever the Watchman was watching for wasn't much of a concern to us kids. We just wanted to find him, to see him, to solve his mystery. We wanted to slay the mythical beast, to save the world. So, we went on epic adventures hunting him. We drew up imaginary maps, configured magic compasses, turned radios into radars, and sharpened tree limbs into swords. We lost ourselves looking for him in the borderlands around town. We scoured the pathless forests, scaled the steepest mountains, and swam the swiftest rivers. We searched for him in town. We broke into abandoned houses, walked the hidden

---

[3] *Who knows where was where people went in those wild, pre-Internet days, when you lost touch with them, when it was still possible to lose touch with them.*

alleyways, and wandered the graveyard in the dead of night. We never did find him.

We conjured him.

***

It happened one Halloween night at Ruby's house. Her parents were gone to who knows where. There was a dozen or so of us kids from around the neighborhood. We'd just finished trick or treating. We were still young enough then to trick or treat, and to believe in ghosts. We sat around the living room, eating and trading the spoils of the day. I'd amassed a trove of Strawberry Starburst. The Strawberry Starburst is the definitive emperor of all Halloween candies. That's a hill I'm willing to die on. I will hear nothing of your chocolate.

Once we'd feasted to excess, we played games. Scary was the theme, of course. We played light as a feather stiff as a board, spoon bend, and Ouija. It was the girls who started the conjuring. They were trying to conjure up their future husbands with this ludicrous ritual. First, they'd darken the whole house, then walk backward upstairs with a candle, into Ruby's bedroom, where her full-length mirror stood. They'd turn to the mirror, blow out the candle, and chant.

On Halloween look in the glass
Your future husbands face will pass

After a few chants, they'd stare into the mirror until they saw something. They always saw something. Usually took a few minutes. Usually a future husband. I don't doubt they saw things in that mirror. Stare in a dark mirror long enough and you're bound to see things that aren't there. It's a scientific fact. It's called the strange face illusion. Eventually, facial features start distorting and disappearing in the mirror. Sometimes other faces appear –animal faces, alien faces, monstrous faces, future husband faces...

After all the husbands had been conjured, we moved on to demons and dead people. Everyone crowded in the bedroom, lights off, candles lit. We started with demons. We successfully conjured Bloody Mary and Candyman. Neither were all that demonical. Candyman was mistaken for someone's future husband. After the demons, we tried out dead people. We conjured John Lennon, Darth Vader, Captain Hook, and most of the 1927 New York Yankees. Someone swung for the fences and tried to conjure the devil himself. It worked. He looked like a math teacher. That made sense, because I always hated math.

We had some scares, but they were all imagined. The Watchman, on the other hand, was not the least bit imagined. It was Ruby's idea to conjure him, after everyone else had gone home. She dragged me in front of the mirror and started rambling.

Watchman, Scotsman, boogeyman, bluesman.
 Mr. can't haunt a house man,
Couldn't scare a mouse man.
Madman, Batman, bad man.
Is it past your bedtime man?
Watch me watch a Watchman...

She went on like that awhile. I stood next to her, blinking tiredly at myself in the mirror. I was crashing hard from the Strawberry Starburst binge. I was about to leave when we started to see things. At first, our faces began to melt, then spin, but that was nothing unusual. Strange face illusion. Science. But then, something unscientific happened. All the candles in the room blew out at once. Except for the candles in the mirror. Those candles somehow remained lit, as if they belonged to a world of their own, one inside of the mirror. Our reflections disappeared.

Ruby and I stood there, fear-frozen to the carpet. We didn't dare move, afraid the Watchman would notice us. We couldn't see him at first. The mirror was empty and motionless, except for the dancing flames of candlelight. Soon, there came a barely noticeable stir from deep within the mirror. We saw a phantom standing in the distance, looking down at something, his back to us. He lifted his head and turned slowly around, as if he was aware of us.

He saw us then, and we saw him. He looked at us awhile, head tilting in a curious sort of way. At first, he was a faceless shadow, but the more I stared at him, the more his features changed. One second he had the head of skeleton, next a gorgon, then three gorgons, then a massive sphinx head. He laughed a laugh so deep it sounded like it came from the basement. The dark shape of him convulsed as he laughed, growing larger and larger, eventually taking up the whole mirror, making it seem like he was right there in the bedroom with us. He stood there, towering over us, laughing at us, reaching for us.

Then the lights turned on, and poof! He was gone.

"Icarus Isakov! Isn't it time you got home? Your mother must be worried sick."

It was Ruby's mom. She was dressed up as a Pink Lady, from Grease.

Ruby looked at me, pale as a ghost. I looked at her, pale as a goblin ghost. We understood each other. I said goodbye, but it was lie. I walked home, upstairs to my bedroom, straight out my bedroom window, into the branches of a tree, down into the backyard, over the fence into Ruby's backyard, up into the branches of a tree, and in through Ruby's bedroom window.

I slept on her bedroom floor that night; after we chucked the mirror out the window.

In Which I Vanquish the Watchman

Obviously, I vanquish the Watchman. Did you think he vanquished me? If he did, he'd vanquish the rest of this book along with me. This book is short enough as it is.

Here's what happened.

I was up and out the door early the next morning, dreamcatcher in my pocket. I hurried downstairs and through the Inn, with a nod to the bartender. I don't think he realized I was off to the castle. If he did, I'm sure he'd have stopped me, probably talked me out of it. I didn't want to be stopped, because I was unstoppable. I was a white goblin knight on his way to rescue a captive princess from some castle-dwelling evil spirit, or monster, or Watchman.

Why was I so confident, you ask? Good question. It was the dreamcatcher. It felt like it held some secret power, like a sword sheathed at my side. The thing about carrying a sword around is you feel pretty much invincible. Doesn't matter if you aren't invincible, or if you don't know how to use a sword. Doesn't matter if the sword isn't a sword, or if you're a scrawny goblin like me. With a sword, you *are a* swordsman.

I marched through downtown on my way to the castle looking all sorts of dangerous. Unfortunately, downtown was completely empty, with no one to admire such a fine specimen of a goblin champion. I imagined I looked like one of those murderous goblins you read about in old legends, all muscly and gritty, leathery skin, the cut of my overall jib immensely intimidating. The Watchman would give me no trouble, none whatsoever.

The castle looked formidable, like something out of Sleeping Beauty, though a tad more sleepy than beautiful. Not that it was ugly. It looked like your run-of-the-mill fairytale castle. There were soaring stone ramparts, watchtowers with arrow slits, and a great keep rising from deep within. The castle sat so near to the mountains behind it you'd have thought it was chiseled out of the rock itself. There was no sign of life anywhere in or around it.

My road led to the castle gatehouse, a front door of sorts, where I'd heard the Watchman kept his watch. The gatehouse itself was a small stone fortress about two stories high, shorter than the adjoining castle walls. There were two towers on each side of the gatehouse meant for guards to stand watch on, though I didn't see any. A dark pathway closed off by a portcullis led through the center of the gatehouse.

THE IMAGINED HOMECOMING OF ICARUS ISAKOV

I approached the gatehouse slowly, hand firmly on the dreamcatcher. There was no one to be seen, nothing to be heard, either. The silence was too silent. Until it wasn't.

"CAWWWWWWWWW!"

A crow cawed, perched high above on the castle walls, scaring the totality of shit out of me. Funny that little caw was all it took to change me from goblin warrior back to goblin banker. All my confidence was lost in an instant. What in actual hell was I doing? As I wondered what that might be, I for some reason kept walking forward.

I was nearly at the gatehouse when the portcullis gate slowly lifted. As it did, it made this horrifying clickety-click sound. It was the same clickety-click you hear when you're riding a roller coaster slowly up to its highest height, before it dives down at a million miles per hour, sending your stomach into your throat. Despite the fact I wasn't riding a roller coaster, the clickety-click had the same effect, sending my stomach up into the vicinity of my clavicle.

Clickety-click, click, click...

Then the clickety-click stopped, replaced with the nervous chatter of my teeth. The gate was then fully open. From the shadows under the archway emerged another shadow. I expected the Watchman, big as the mountain itself, something in the general shape of hell, with eyes shooting forth flame and teeth like Jaws. I pictured him carrying an arsenal of swords, spears, and scimitars to eviscerate me with. Maybe a bazooka for good measure.

Then I saw him.

Only it wasn't him. It was a gnome. No taller than a daisy.

"Good day." The gnome tipped his cap to me, strolling on by like any old gnome in the street. And that was it. I saw no sight of the Watchman that day.

Yes, you could argue the title of this chapter was misleading, that I didn't exactly vanquish the Watchman. But who knows? It could be that he spontaneously combusted at the sight of me. More likely he wasn't home. Or maybe he never existed in the first place. Maybe he was a case of small-town gossip gone wild. Whatever the case, I was well pleased to have avoided him.

So much for the dreamcatcher. It was useless, or so I thought.

***

I passed underneath the dark archway of the gatehouse into a glowing courtyard. There were perfectly trimmed, bright green hedges lining red brick walkways. A great fountain of pink marble rose from the middle. There was every color flower, everywhere. A handful of stone gargoyles perched about. They were my only company. There was no one else to be seen.

I made my way through the courtyard toward the keep on the far side. If anyone was anywhere, it would be there. The keep looked like one of those massive and mysterious medieval cathedrals, either supremely evil or whatever the opposite of supremely evil is. Two tall arched doors of a dark, gleaming wood with golden strap hinges made me think there was something important inside, something unexpected. There was.

Inside was unexpectedly empty.

There was nothing, no kings, queens, princes, or princesses. There weren't any castle-goers period. Even stranger, there were no royal furnishings. No thrones, coats of arms, suits of armor, magical mirrors, tapestries, none of that. The great hall was greatly empty. The adjoining halls, bedchambers, a kitchen, bathrooms, they were all just as empty. The place was even empty of sound. My footsteps made war on the silence, each step an explosion of echoes. The fading afternoon light pouring in through the open-air windows was my only company.

The castle was a mystery. Who built it, and why? Where were they, where was anyone? Why was it so empty? What purpose could an empty castle possibly serve? I wandered the castle grounds for answers, for hours. I explored everything, every closet of every bedchamber, every inch of every rampart, every storeroom, cellar, every larder. Then I explored it all again. Nothing. My only clue was the fact there were no clues. It was a castle of fantasy, of imagination only.

I looked down over the town below from high above on the battlements. It was hardly more alive than the castle. Lights flickered on here and there like dying embers from a once bright fire. The late afternoon was transforming into one of those dark and stormy nights you're always hearing about. The rain was close. I could smell it, a fragrant flashback from when I was a kid. I always wondered what it was that made rain smell so good.

I hurried from the castle in a race against the storm. I wasn't far from the Inn when a clap of thunder unleashed a deluge for the ages. The first raindrops were more buckets than drops. I ran that last short stretch up the hill to the Inn front door as fast as I could, but there was no point. In a matter of seconds I was bedraggled, heel to horns.

I sloshed up the stairs to my room. After a quick dry off and change, I came back down to the tavern for dinner. Place was busy. There were no tables available, so I bellied up to the bar. My bartender was waiting for me.

"I'm a starved goblin. What's on the menu tonight?"

"Fresh fish from our very own Rockville River. How does that suit your fancy?"

"Suitably. Tell me more."

"We're serving a unique, dual-purpose fish tonight. This wholesome fish fills your stomach, *and* your memory. May I recommend one particular entree for you, sir?"

"You may."

"Certainly. I suggest the Skinny-Dipping Dogfish. We poach the freshly-caught fish in our own simmering seasons from long ago, add a dash of thyme, a hint of lost time, and voila!"

"Lovely. I'll take it, and a fancy beer while you're at it."

Felt like I deserved a fancy beer while he was at it.

He served me my fancy beer, then dinner. The fish looked and tasted probably more spectacular than it was, since I hadn't eaten all day. It was mildly fishy, like trout or halibut. There were sides of vegetables, but also something else, some hardly noticeable, yet familiar flavor within the fish itself. It wasn't until I'd gotten down to the last few bites when I realized what the flavor was.

It was the river itself.

Night Swimming with Goblins

I'm a teenaged goblin, drowning in the throes of puberty, along with all my friends, and Ruby.

We pass the summer night together behind a little farmhouse in a tomato garden, sitting on haystacks around a bonfire. We sip from glass jars of beer and lemonade, laughing, touching, the best of us kissing. Stars circle magically overhead. The night so far has been a perfect one. Problem is, there's little left to the night. Although the night is ending, no one is in the least bit tired. We are the opposite of tired. We are restless.

What to do?

On any other night, the night would end. Cigarettes put out. Drinks poured on the fire. Hugs given. Hands shaken. We would all go our own way, home to bed, maybe alone, maybe not. Worried parents, laying half-awake in bed, would hear the front door creak open, the footsteps to the bedroom, and be relieved. Soon, everyone would be sleeping peacefully. The night would pass quietly, never to return. That was how any other night ended.

But, this wasn't any other night. This was a night for night swimming.

The conditions that night were just right for night swimming. The night was one of those strange midsummer ones –infinite space above, finite time below, where the blurring of fantasy and reality make anything possible. It was one of those nights where you'd trade a single minute more for the whole next day, where you'd sacrifice anything for the night to go on indefinitely. Night swimming is a perfect means of accomplishing just that. Night swimming doesn't just buy time; it stops it.

So, in the tomato garden around the little fire, the night didn't end as it normally would. Towards the end of it, sometime after midnight, when the sexual tension in the air had thickened to a point when something must absolutely be done about it, someone suggested a stroll under the summer stars, to the river, for a swim. It was only a mile away, after all. The fire was dwindling after all. We had nothing else to do after all.

The idea was declared the most brilliant one in the history of the universe. We hurried to leave the garden, rushing excitedly here and there, gathering what little we needed, swarming out of the back gate like a band of escaped mental patients. Clouds gathered overhead as we walked together across a prairie meadow toward the woods in the distance. The night was still dotted with fireflies, but not your usual florescent fireflies. The fireflies in goblin country glow in every sort of color you can think of. They congregated closest to the woods, blinking rainbow, dressing the trees in Christmas lights early. It was strange to see fireflies that late into the night. I guess they also refused to let the night end.

About halfway across the meadow, a whoosh of wind surprised us. Thunder grumbled. Lightning flashed on the horizon. That familiar scent of rain filled the air. A storm would soon be joining us. No matter. There was no turning back, not if a monsoon presented itself. We hurried along, made more excited than ever at the approaching storm, and the swim.

The rain waited until we were under the trees so that we were mostly sheltered from it, at least until we reached the river. We skipped, hopped, and staggered in a wobbly single file line down a narrow trail, which wound around trees and bushes, but kept on steadily toward the river. Lightning flashed more frequently the further we walked, helping us to navigate the path, and exposing the gnarled, gnomish faces of the trees. They stared amazedly at us as we passed them by, because we truly were amazing.

Walking on, between the sounds of our own voices and the storm, we heard the flow of the river and knew we were close. The trail climbed steeply at its end. One by one, we reached the hilly boundary of the woods, where we looked down on the shadowy, fast-flowing river. The water was indistinguishable from the rainy night sky. You could hardly see it, but we knew it was there.

The sight of the river sent us all into a frenzy. We raced to strip our clothes off, flinging them on tree branches as we ran, stumbled, and dove maniacally in the river, looking like that same band of escaped mental patients from the garden. Seconds from when we'd arrived at the river, we were up to our necks in it. A few of the boldest were totally naked, but most of us kept our underwear on. Rain poured, thunder rolled, and lightning struck, the now full-blown storm adding to the reckless scene.

The river served as one of the few places of total freedom for us. In that secluded place, free from parents, teachers, rules, and structure, we became our true, romantic selves. We were water sprites, sea serpents, and vampire squids. We were mermaids, long suffocated on dry land, returned home, drunk on water. We were wild animals, without a yesterday or tomorrow, without a single regret or worry, for one of the last times in our lives. Splashes and waves transformed into the tentacles of some monstrous Kraken, breaking harmlessly on our shoulders. The rain began pouring so hard at one point it was hard to separate the water below from the water above. All you could hear was water and laughter. Occasionally, a lightning flash would rent the sky from top to bottom, unleashing electrical demons throughout the air, who joined in the mayhem. The lightning was of no concern to

STEVE WILEY

us because we were anything we wanted to be. Among other things, we were invincible.

Ruby was one of those fully naked ones, a little girl no more, dancing and singing in the water like a small-town siren. I was a drunken sailor in his tighty-whities. She lured me into her arms, far out in the middle of the river, where no one could see us. She kissed me there for the first time, as we drifted away from the party along with the current. We kissed, and drifted, without noticing we were drifting at all because the only thing worth noticing was each other. From then on, Ruby was something altogether different to me, something much more complicated than the girl next door.

Cabaret of Yesterday

Back to the Inn.

After the delicious, Skinny-Dipping Dogfish recollected for me my skinny-dipping days, I went upstairs to my room to sleep. I was exhausted from the trip. The search for Ruby had been a strange one, taking me from the deepness of old wishing wells to the highest of castle ramparts, yet turned up nothing. The only place I could find Ruby was in the past, in all those childhood memories conjured by the Forgetful Faun Inn.

I slept the better part of the next day, before doing some aimless wandering about town –nothing spectacular to report from that. I had a glass with old O'Hagan, where I laughed. I had a swing at the old playground, where I cried. I had a scare passing by the old graveyard. Thought I saw a ghost digging himself out of a grave. Turned out to be a gravedigger digging himself into one. I made a mental note to visit my parents in the graveyard before I left town.

I returned to the Inn late that afternoon, hoping for no more than an uneventful evening to complete my ordinary day. I'd eat a nice dinner, drink fancy beer, make a new friend or friends, play darts or pool, engage in philosophical pub talk with the bartender, and all that sort of normalcy. I just wanted a normal night. As you'd guess by now, normal was out of the question. You wouldn't be reading this story if it was ordinary.

***

The Inn that night was busier than I'd thought possible. There were dark elves, light elves, goblins, hobgoblins, wood trolls, river trolls, mountain dwarves, hill dwarves, drunk dwarves, girls, guys, and golems. The reclusive town vampire was even there. It seemed like the whole remaining population of the town was at the bar that night. But why?

I sought the bartender for answers, as one does. He was where he always was, concocting his enchanted concoctions behind the bar. He was busier than ever serving the crowd, so it took a few minutes to flag him down.

"Evening! May I have one pint of something and the reason I can hardly walk in here?"

"One pint of something coming right up. As for the reason you can hardly walk in here, that would be the jukebox over yonder."

"Sorry, did you say *the jukebox over yonder*?"

"Yes, and it's no ordinary jukebox. See it, next to the fireplace?"

Over yonder was indeed a jukebox. Picture the

grooviest jukebox[4] you ever saw, and you might be picturing something like this jukebox. This one was a tall, wide cabinet of a vintage music machine, complete with shiny hardwood veneers and glowing rainbow-colored bubble tubes percolating around the top. It had a latticed grille of what looked like the God Pan playing his pipes over the main middle speaker. The jukebox looked like it played magic music, and it did.

"Some jukebox. What does it play?"

The bartender served me my pint of something.

"It plays the past. You drop a coin in, the jukebox registers the year on the coin, along with the dropper of the coin, then transports the whole bar to somewhere from the year of the coin, somewhere the dropper intended to revisit. Turns the whole bar into a kind of impromptu cabaret for the night. It's all quite entertaining. Look! It's starting."

The bar quieted. A path cleared to the jukebox. Through that path walked the oldest old crone I ever saw. She was all skin and bones below a raggedy, backward shift dress. She was mostly bald, with only a few strands of white hanging here or there. I felt sorry for her. Everyone did.

The whole bar watched her as she leaned tiredly against jukebox. She drew a deep breath, exhausted from standing, from living. She pulled a silver coin from her pocket and held

---

[4] If you pictured a digital, touch screen jukebox, I am sad for you.

it up to the light. She squinted up at it, making certain of the year, before dropping it in the jukebox. The coin echoed like a tear in the fabric of time as it tumbled through the jukebox.

Quick as you read this, the old woman was shrouded in mist, followed by the rest of the bar. When the fog cleared, the bar as I knew it was gone, replaced with a school gymnasium, where a school dance was taking place. The chandelier was replaced with a silver disco ball. The mahogany bar became a plastic table. Beer and peanuts turned to punch and crackers. The gym was crowded with black Buddy Holly glasses and red Marilyn Monroe lipstick. None wore shoes as they bunny hopped and jived on the gym floor, so as not to scratch it.

I was at a sock hop.

The only thing that remained unchanged was the jukebox. The old crone stood near it, old crone no more. Where she once stood was the pink poodle skirt-wearing teenage pixie she once was. She didn't stand there long, smiling and dancing, golden pigtails bouncing to music too old for me to recognize. It sounded like something genuine, from the dawn of rock and roll.

I followed the old crone turned pixie as she whirled around the gymnasium. She was loving it, but I could tell there was something missing. It seemed to me she was looking for some special someone. Every time a slow song came on, she weaved in and out of slow-dancing couples, looking for some lost dance partner she could never seem to find.

The jukebox played on. I sensed when the music ended the sock hop would also end. After a few slow songs had played, she started to get more frantic in her search. I guess she knew she would turn back into an old pumpkin once the jukebox stopped playing, once the clock struck midnight. Still, she had no luck finding whoever she was looking for. She collapsed onto the bleachers, face in her hands.

I was about to drag her onto the dance floor myself when I felt a draft from the gymnasium door. Someone had joined the party late. Complete with pompadour hair and letterman's jacket, there was the goblin greaser our pixie was hoping for. He rescued her from the bleachers, leading her onto the dance floor just in time for the last song.

> *Moon river, wider than a mile*
> *I'm crossing you in style someday*
> *Oh, dream maker*
> *You heartbreaker*
> *Where ever you're going, I'm going your way*
> *Two drifters off to see the world*
> *There's such a lot of world to see*
> *We're after the same rainbow's end*
> *Waiting round the bend*
> *My huckleberry friend*
> *Moon river and me*

They danced like they'd danced before, in another life. They kissed that same way. Soon, the jukebox fell silent, and the gym lights dimmed. When everything else was dark, I could still see the faint silver twinkle from the disco ball.

When the lights turned back on, they were bar lights.

***

"One creamy pint of porter and two chewy fingers of whiskey, please?" I asked the bartender.

The thing about time traveling in a bar is it puts you in a mood for drinking, *excessively*. Maybe it was the anticipation or just my weak goblin nerves. Whatever it was, I was putting them back like a goblin Winston Churchill.

Across the Inn, a druid was sizing the jukebox up. He was a big green fella with a weather-beaten, tree-lichen-covered face under a thick red beard and long hair of colorful autumn leaves. Out of his head sprouted two giant antlers. He cut quite the woodsy figure. Hard to imagine where this character would be taking us.

The bar quietly watched as he dug around his pocket for change, pulling a shiny chunk out and into his wicker basket of a hand. He picked through the silver and gold, looking for a coin with a certain date. I'd had another whole pint of porter before he finally found the one he wanted. He held the coin high for all to see, a sort of ritualistic pronouncement, before dropping it in the jukebox.

The moment he dropped the coin in, a gale-force wind burst through the bar, blowing everything away in seconds.

I was sent flying off my barstool. First thing I noticed when I rose was the Inn, or lack thereof. It was gone entirely, the whole place blown to Oz. I was outside. I gazed up to where the bar ceiling had been into an unobstructed, star-filled sky. Serpents of stardust slithered in and around masses of glowing galaxy, and it seemed to me every single stitch of the universe was revealed in a single glance up. Living in the city, I'd not seen so many stars in forever. Looking up at them, I felt cured of commerce.

All around me, where the Inn had been, the hills were filled with townsfolk. I knew straight away I was at the town's annual summer festival. Carnival grounds glowed golden nearer to Main Street. Little monsters ran wild with black cats and bottle rockets. Fairies chased goblins with sparklers. Goblins chased fairies with bang snaps. Dads drank Budweiser. Moms smoked Newports. They all wore cut-off jeans. That sulfuric, floral scent of summer filled the air.

The jukebox played a steady stream of power ballads, all with heavy doses of synthesizer and electric guitar. I roamed the hills a while, bobbing my head to the gated reverb, *a-with the record selection and the mirror's reflection*, occasionally dancing with myself. And I can't even dance. Soon I happened upon a much smaller version of the druid, with a group of his friends. The group had taken ownership of one particularly tall hill, where they played king of the hill. Druids literally worshipped hills, so it was an all too common game for them.

I sat down in an empty folding chair and watched the game. It was an entertaining one. At first, a young ogre was king. He was a merciless monarch. He used his size and strength to club and kick challengers away. He was dethroned by a centaur, who punted him off the hilltop with a bucking that would have killed anyone smaller. The centaur's reign on the hill-throne lasted only a few seconds before he was swarmed by a pack of goblins. After that, the hill government changed from an absolute monarchy to pure anarchy. The goblins fought amongst themselves a while until one great goblin emerged victoriously and the monarchy was restored. The great goblin stood on top of the hill, and none dare challenge him, until the druid. He must have cast some druidic spell, because when the great goblin charged down at him, he charged straight past him, off into the distance like a lunatic. The druid stood on the hill, the final king of it.

Just then, a deafening explosion sounded overhead. I looked up, along with the rest of the town. The explosion was an aerial mortar, the signal for the big fireworks show to start.

The game abruptly stopped. The combatants turned friends again, as they scurried to the top of the hill where they sat together, staring up at the magic. Instead of watching the fireworks, I found myself watching the kids watch the fireworks. If you ever find yourself watching kids watch fireworks, congratulations because you've officially grown up. I couldn't help but be mesmerized at how awe-struck they all were, their faces unmoving, their changing skin colors with the changing bursts of colors above.

In the middle of it all, the druid stood up, pointing his finger to the sky. His finger glowed faintly at first, in an E.T. sort of way. Slowly though, the finger became brighter and brighter, until it exploded in sporadic bursts of green rockets, like a roman candle. He pointed it straight up into the fireworks show, which was about to reach its climax. When it did, the night was overcome by a past-devouring fog, which rolled over the hills and returned us all to the Inn.

***

"Beer and a shot, please."

The liquor ran like water down my parched throat that night. I couldn't get enough. I drank and wondered where the jukebox would take us next, then drank some more.

Making his way to the jukebox was the town vampire. I knew the sight of him. Everyone knew the sight of him. He looked the same as he always did - dusty, dodgy, dangerous. Typical vampire. The crowd cleared away from him like he had the plague. The town vampire is sort of like the town drunk. No kid wants to be the town drunk when they grow up; it just sort of happens. When it does, no one wants to be near you, or have anything to do with you.

I didn't see the town vampire drop his coin in, but he must have because before I knew it, I was out of the bar and into a living room. It didn't look like a vampire living room at all. It looked like an ordinary living room, albeit an old, old-fashioned one. Two ordinary adults, a man and woman, entered from an adjacent room. The man wore an army green service uniform. The woman wore a nightgown. The town vampire was nowhere to be seen.

The man and woman began searching the living room for something, or someone. They turned the room upside down, looking worried as they did, but found nothing. They were standing together in the center of the room, looking hopelessly confused, when a camouflage duffel bag that had been resting against the wall tumbled over. Out of the bag rolled a small boy, maybe seven years old. The boy was the town vampire, before he was the town vampire. The man was his father, the lady his mother. This was the town vampire's family. The boy was hiding in the duffel bag because his father was leaving, and he wanted to go with him. I couldn't see the jukebox anywhere, but I could hear it. It sounded like an antique radio. The song came out so softly and staticky, I could hardly make out the words.

My heart is sad, and I'm in sorrow
For the only one I love

With the boy found, his father continued about the house, packing for his trip. The boy clung to his father's ankle the whole while. The father didn't seem bothered by it.

The mother did seem bothered by it. She paced in circles around the living room, dusting nervously, checking her wristwatch every so often. I got the sense the father was going to a dangerous place, a place there was no returning from.

When shall I see him, oh, no, never
Till I meet him in heaven above

The father pried the boy from his leg as he sat down on the couch to put on his boots. He rose from the couch and draped himself in an oversized, army green pea coat, then proceeded to the front door, where his wife waited for him. The boy had reattached himself to his father's leg and refused to let go. After his mother pulled the boy off, the father kissed and hugged them both, tossed the duffel bag over his shoulder, put on a peaked hat from the coat rack, and walked out the door. A few snowflakes blew in before the door closed behind him.

Oh, bury me under the weeping willow
Yes, under the weeping willow tree
So he may know where I am sleeping
And perhaps he will weep for me

The boy's mother comforted him as he sobbed in her lap on the couch. She whispered something into his ear, and he smiled through the tears. She picked him up, and holding him by the wrists, spun his little body around in circles. The dizziness made the boy happy. She whirled him around, again and again. I could hear them laughing over the music until the lights in the living room dimmed, and the jukebox quieted.

***

I was one of the very last at the bar that night. Yes, I was drunk as a goblin fiddler, but that's not the point. The last one at the bar has a reason for being the last one at the bar. Mine was the jukebox. I wanted a turn. Of course, I wanted to go somewhere I just wasn't sure where. If you could revisit any occasion from your past, if only for a little while, where would you go?

"What are you waiting for?" The bartender was closing shop and reading my mind.

"I'm all out of change." I was. Who the hell carries change around?

"Here." The bartender flipped me a gold coin. It hit me in the forehead and fell to the floor. My reflexes were nonexistent. I was so drunk I could hardly stand.

"Thanks."

I pocketed the coin, drank what was left from my glass, and proceeded to the magical jukebox. I barely made it there. The room was spinning. I dropped the bartender's coin in without even looking at the date. I leaned on the jukebox, pleading for it to play *Freebird*. In my drunken stupor, I'd forgotten the sort of jukebox I was dealing with. The last thing I remember was the grandfather clock, snorting pixie dust off the table next to me. The bartender laughed at us both.

The Last Cassette

Next thing I remembered was the last cassette.

The last cassette played in the last Buick Skylark, on the last day of high school, through a haze of the last guilt-free cigarette smoke ever smoked. The Buick Skylark was loaded with talking, touching, tippling eighteen-year-olds. The Buick Skylark was an utter shit-box, but it was also lovely. It was a swerving celebration of summer, featuring the finest in magnetic tape music.

Artie the Anthropomorph was behind the wheel. We called Artie that because we had no idea what he actually was. He claimed to be French, but there was no way. He didn't look even remotely human. He looked like a hairless Wookiee. Riding next to him in the front passenger seat was one Danny Davison. Danny was the quintessential lost boy. No one was waiting up for him at home, if he even had one. The Skylark was his home that night. How Ruby and I wound up together in the backseat I couldn't say, but there we were, first sitting, then laying across the backseat, then rolling onto the floor. More on that shortly.

When the last cassette played, the night was coming to

an end. Chirping birds tried to alert us of that fact, as the few final stars faded over Rockville. We paid the birds and brightening sky no mind. Time was of no consequence. We had so much time there was no point in even keeping track of it. We had the whole summer before us, and summer for a kid is infinite.

We drove and celebrated on, determined to end the night not when it was over for everyone else, but when we decided it should end, for us. We all agreed a proper ending would be on the road, with the sunrise. So, we sped eastward down a lonely interstate. The windows were rolled down, the morning wind an opening act for whatever the old cassette player had in store.

"In the words of Robert Anthony Plant, I'm in the mood for a melody." Ruby commanded, being the commander in the car. The rest of us were just grunts, along for the ride.

Artie blindly plucked the last cassette from the center console and pushed it into the tape player. Don't ask me what the album or the song was. It would have sounded different for you. It sounded different for all of us that night. I know it did, because the moment the music started, I felt the strange sensation of hearing it from the ears of each of the passengers.

Artie heard the last cassette like a river song. The highway was a winding, fast-flowing river, and he was a moonlight sailor. The farmhouses on each side passed like colorful rushes along some countryside stream. He was blazing down the waterway, steering with one hand, dexterously smoking hash from a tiny roach clip with the other. He was high, far too high to be driving. The headlights from the cars driving in the opposite direction took the shape of strange river monsters, scowling and laughing at him as they whizzed past. Artie scowled and laughed back. When the river rose, he felt as though the Buick Skylark might transform into a real skylark, soaring off into the sky, off between the morning and the night. He drank the smoke in deep, feeling calm and glad and dizzy, as a jingle of bar chimes played from the last cassette.

For Danny riding shotgun, the last cassette played a lullaby. The night for him had been the longest, and he was by far the drunkest. He was always the drunkest. He rested his head on the window, his curly brown hair blown straight back, his hand outside the window, soaring up and down like a bird in the wind. Danny was in that limbo state of consciousness, neither fully awake nor fully asleep. The singer's voice rang crackly and distant through the cheap car speakers, sounding like a noise already in the past. It only took a few of the last cassette lyrics to put Danny entirely to sleep, where he dreamed a boyish dream of a pretty girl. She pedaled through the sky on a flying bicycle, hiking up her skirt, singing to him from the stars above. She sang the lyrics of the song playing on the last cassette. Danny watched and listened, and was happy. He slept with a smile on his face and hoped never to wake again.

For Ruby and I, the last cassette played a song that seemed to have been recorded solely for our use, as we made out in the backseat. Ruby tasted like strawberries. I tasted less sweet, but just good enough for the backseat of a Buick Skylark. As Artie sped and swerved down the highway, we did our best to remain still, clutching seats, doors, and each other, until we finally flopped down on top of one another across the back seat, where we no longer minded the sharp turns. We never kissed again after that night, but anytime that song from the last cassette played afterward, it evoked the memory of that last kiss.

We made it to where we were going that night, to the sunrise. The sunrise sounded like a better idea than it actually turned out to be. It felt offensively bright, as it tends to when you've been up all night. Artie took his sweet time driving all of us home. That was fine. I wasn't in any rush. I had all the vastness of a childhood summer ahead of me. We all did.

Of course, there were other cassettes played after that last one, but never out of necessity. CD replaced cassette, then digital replaced CD. Eventually, something will replace digital, and people will miss it like they miss everything once loved, even when replaced with something better. People listen to cassettes nowadays for the same reason they listen to records. They listen not for a better sound, but a lost one.

Chance Encounters

I woke up disgracefully late the next morning.

I looked like the Grinch. I was an avocado shade of green. My skin was all sunken and tight. My arms and legs dangled from the sides of my bed like rotten twigs. My bloodshot eyes were so red they looked filled with undigested red wine. Maybe they were. I was coping with a real-life hangover. I spent the better part of the morning rehydrating, fending off panic attacks, questioning my existence. I never pray, but I prayed that morning. I prayed to the goblin Gods for the pain to go away. I promised them I'd never drink again. You know the routine.

Eventually, I managed to wash up and hobble downstairs to the bar for some much-needed sustenance. It was noiseless compared to the night before. The jukebox was nowhere to be seen. There were only a handful of patrons. The bartender was, of course, working. He mixed me up this fantastical potion that cured most of my hangover symptoms the instant I gulped it down. That's true wizardry, curing a hangover. Albus Dumbledore never cured a hangover.

THE IMAGINED HOMECOMING OF ICARUS ISAKOV

I ate a little something, then headed out to get the blood pumping. The day was a cool, misty one, perfectly suited for a visit to mom and dad at the old graveyard. The old graveyard was so utterly an old graveyard you'd mistake yourself for dead just passing through it. It was the only one in town, founded when the town was. I wondered how well it was kept up, what with the town mostly abandoned and all. With no one left to die, does a graveyard go out of business? I'd find out.

As expected, the town that day was a ghost town, dead as any graveyard. I hardly noticed the change of scenery when I walked through the rusty cemetery gates. You could see no one had tended the grounds in forever. The grass was all uncut, some of the graves drowning in it. The mausoleums were suffocated with wild ivy. The stone trails were covered in weeds, the tree branches hanging low over them like those beaded, hippie door curtains. Stray patches of fog crept up and down the green hills of headstones like roaming clumps of spirits.

I made my way through the wet fields, deep into the heart of the graveyard, toward where I guessed my family was buried. I say *guessed* because I was. I hadn't been there in years. The last time I was, it looked much different. Back then, I could see where the paths twisted and turned. Now, I was navigating an endless sea of graves and greenery.

I wandered up and down the hills awhile, half-lost, until I came upon a familiar landmark - this stubby, crumbling stone wall, which led even deeper into the graveyard. I knew if I followed that stone wall, I should eventually run into the cemetery chapel, and a little further on, the family plot. So, I walked on, the drizzle thickening to a soft, steady rain.

Up to that day, I never once believed in ghosts. I was a staunch materialist. I believed in science, in testability. Ghosts were the stuff of fantasy, of make-believe. Well, I changed my stance on ghosts that day. I had no choice. The whole scene was just too ghostly. The weather was ghostly. The trees and plants were ghostly. The graves were ghostly. All that ghostliness made my imagination ghostly. I started seeing and hearing things. I saw apparitions lurking within the clouds of fog. I heard banshees whistling through the wind and rain. I walked light as a goblin ballerina, scared a wight might rise from the ground and pull me under. I wouldn't have been the least bit surprised to run into a ghost out for a stroll.

Then I did.

He was sitting on the stone wall up ahead of me, dangling his legs, a little notebook in one hand, a glass of something in the other. I could tell he was a ghost straight away, the way he looked so at home. He looked like the ghost of a young, beardless dwarf. He tipped his cap to me as I walked up. He wasn't the least bit scary. In fact, he was friendly.

"Great day to be a ghost," said the ghost.

"Great day to be a goblin," I said.

He leaped off the wall in surprise.

"I'll be damned, if I wasn't already damned! What brings a living, breathing soul to the graveyard?"

"The usual. On my way to visit the Isakov clan."

"Lovely, lovely. Pleasure to meet you. I'm Bobby McGee."

"Icarus Isakov. Pleasure's all mine."

"Care for a sip of spirits?" He held his glass up, catching rain drops with it. "Look at me, a spirit drinking spirits. It's like supernatural cannibalism, eh? I'm too dead to care, and they say you're only dead once, right?"

"So they say."

"They do. Everyone but the Hindus, that is."

"I've never met a ghost. May I ask how you got in the ghosting business?"

"Oh, the usual way. It was a morphine shot, black tar heroin I think it was, that did it. When I first shot up, I thought I was in a temporary blackout of sorts. Turned out to be more permanent than that. They found my body in Willingham Fountain..."

"I'm sorry." Willingham Fountain was smack dab in the center of town. Must have been the headline of the century in the Rockville Reader.

"Don't be sorry. I don't envy the living, not anymore. I think the Internet ruined it for me."

"Hard to disagree with that."

133

"Now I mostly write. I died obituary-less, so writing my own right now. Wanna hear it?"

"Yes, certainly. Who doesn't love a good obituary?"

He cleared his throat and read from his notebook.

"Ok, here goes."

An overdose is like a modern-day fairy tale,
With mermaids, dragons, and knights in chainmail.
The truth of that is plain to see,
In the peculiar case of Bobby McGee.

Bobby was locally grown in the ruby city,
Newly a man, baby faced and pretty.
He was a lonely bachelor, shy as a pearl,
So shy in fact, he'd not yet kissed a girl.

That night began under a cockeyed moon,
It was martinis up in the local saloon.
One led to two,
Two led to three,
Until there was a drunken Bobby McGee.

Then she strolled in wearing a corset bra,
Cupid overhead, Bobby swore he saw.
When she said, "How cute a name is McGee?"
Bobby was in love, easy as one two three.

THE IMAGINED HOMECOMING OF ICARUS ISAKOV

She introduced herself as The Bee Charmer,
And might he be her knight in shining armor?
They drank until their fill was had.
They drank until it tasted bad.

She said, "Why not go somewhere for tastier sips?"
He'd follow her to hell for a kiss from those lips.
He stumbled after her across the bar room floor,
Feeling more like flying as they walked out the door.

The two rode his red pickup like a firedrake,
Soaring (bumpily) toward daybreak.
Soon they arrived, she with a hidden heroic gram,
To the center of town, the fountain of Willingham.

The fountain sparkled below in ghostly hues,
Wind shook the trees with a sound like the blues.
Sitting together there at the edge of the abyss,
Young Bobby McGee finally got his first kiss.

She wrapped his wrist in a tie dye tourniquet,
And loaded black tar into a syringe, bit by bit,
Sinking the needle through his peach fuzz,
Bobby felt his head explode with a mighty buzz.

Overdosed Bobby fell and fell and fell and fell,
Straight through the bottom of a wishing well.

A mermaid swam by checking her wristwatch.
The water tasted like psychedelic butterscotch.

The last he heard was she who charmed a bee,
Singing what sounded like Mr. Jones and Me.
His ghost flew over the town with a moonlight tan,
You'd have thought the specter a lost Peter Pan.

A body in Willingham, police thought queer.
The heartbeat of course, they could not hear.
Bobby wore the strangest smile of hypnotic bliss,
With bruising on one arm's vein shaped like a kiss.

An overdose is like a modern-day fairy tale,
With mermaids, dragons, and knights in chainmail.
The truth of that is plain to see,
In the peculiar case of Bobby McGee.

I gave him a round of applause.

He thanked me and we exchanged pleasantries awhile longer. He was a talkative one, probably could have talked himself to death a second time. I told him I'd best be getting on before it got dark. I might encounter some less congenial ghosts after dark.

"That you might, I won't deny it. Answer me one question, before you go. What's it like to kiss somebody. I mean really kiss somebody. I never tried it, as you could tell from my obit."

"Kisses? I'd say kisses are like birthdays, each new one a little different, a little less important than the last. Those first ones though, those are indescribable. I've never shot heroin, but I imagine those first few kisses might be something like heroin."

He shook his head and smiled.

"I'll be damned, if I wasn't already damned."

***

I continued deeper in the graveyard, following the stone wall, until I ran into the chapel I'd been looking for. It looked about ready to collapse. Black mold crawled up the sides, covering the once white exterior like a cancer. The stained-glass windows were surprisingly unbroken. They looked brighter than ever above the mold and mist. Just beyond the chapel, I saw the hill I was looking for and the Isakov plot.

I walked up the hill, passed my long-dead ancestors to my more recently dead ones nearer the top. My parent's graves were up there. No sign of them though. No sign of any ghosts whatsoever. Wasn't much to do, so I did those things you do at graveyards. I sulked around a bit, clearing overgrowth from headstones and then staring at headstones, remembering people on headstones, and getting sad remembering people on headstones. That sort of thing.

The grass on top of the hill was tall and wet and wavy. After wandering around only a little while up there, my pants were drenched. I found that as good a reason as any to leave so headed back down the way I came. Now that I had my bearings, I decided to take a shortcut back to the graveyard entrance. It would take me away from any trails, chapels, or stone walls, straight across a plain of tombstones.

The shortcut took me through some of the oldest graves in the cemetery. Most of them were so old you could hardly make out the names or dates on them. One patch of graves was so moss and algae covered they looked indistinguishable from the green grass below. Here and there I would encounter patches of more recent headstones. I found myself walking along one especially new row of graves, not ten years old by the look of them. I read the names as I passed each grave by, recognizing more than a few. There was Sheriff Griffin the gryphon, Ezekiel the butcher, Mike the manticore mechanic, Principal Peryton, Mayor Mandrake and his wife, Alicorn the accountant, and plenty more.

Then I saw the one.

I think I was looking for it, without realizing I was looking for it. When I saw it, it took all the wind out of me, along with the rest of the graveyard. Time slowed to a crawl, if it moved at all. It has a habit of doing that when you learn the fate of long lost girls next door, or when you just feel like head to toe shit. I found it hard to move for a long time until time sped up again. When it did, there was little for me to do. I wandered in circles around her grave, gathering what few things I could find. I gathered yellow dandelions, the ones she'd smashed against my wrists when we were kids, leaving a bright streak that she'd laugh at, saying a fairy had pissed on me. I picked white dandelion puffs, the ones we'd blow the bulbs off, wishing on them into the wind. I gathered wildflowers, the ones she wore in her hair every spring. I tied them all together with a willow wand and placed them at the base of her grave. It was a modest grave, no more than a foot high. The epitaph was short.

Ruby Rockhollow

Here a Ruby Gleams
Dreaming Better Dreams

Mine Closed!!!

Rockville ran out of rubies last week, putting the future of our beloved town in jeopardy. Reports from Miller Natural Resources Inc., long-time owner of the mine, indicated the mine had been "fully extracted," and that the permanent (yes, permanent) closure was effective last Friday afternoon. Mine employees were informed at the noon whistle Friday.

The village of Rockville was founded when the mine was, some hundreds of years ago, by a nomadic mish-mash of miners. Since that time, we've grown from a temporary mining camp of tents and shacks to the permanent mining community we call home, to the village of families, friends, and neighbors of today. Mining isn't just a job in Rockville; it's a way of life. The mine gave our workers, and our town, a sense of identity, pride, and purpose. To see the mine close will be difficult for all, and brings a tear to this old writer's eye just typing it.

We interviewed one local miner, Jared "Bear" Burress, on the situation. Burress was the last miner, from the last shift at the mine. He had worked at the mine for nearly four *decades. Here's what Burress had to say.*

> *"Only reason you and I is even standing here is them shiny [expletive] rocks found down in the veins of the mountain a thousand years ago. My daddy worked them mines, my daddy's daddy before him, and on and on to the [expletive] bronze age. Rubies, you see, they was our past, present, and future. Now I guess they're just the past, and there ain't no [expletive] future to speak of. At least not here in Rockville."*

The Rockville economy wasn't exactly diverse. It was totally reliant on the mine. The sudden closure of it instantly puts more than half the town out of work, and with so many local businesses dependent on mining money, you can expect many more businesses to close, and many more residents to be out of work in the coming months. Further complicating matters is that most of our miners, especially the oldest, lack any other skills, or the means of learning new skills. Unintended consequence for centuries of doing nothing but mining in this town is a workforce who only know how to do one thing. What careers will our workers transition to, and what career opportunities will remain here in Rockville anyway?

The mine was the beating heart of the town. The red ruby, that precious gemstone, was dearer to Rockville residents than anyone. It was the lifeblood of the town, extracted from the mine since time immemorial. Now, without warning, we've been bled dry.

What will we do? Where will our miners find work? Will Rockville survive without the mine? I don't know the answers to these questions. I don't think anyone does. I'll tell you what I do know.

You don't know what you've got until it's gone.

Chasing Dreams

I sulked my way out of the graveyard, back to the Inn.

First thing I did when I returned to my room was pack. The second thing I did was arrange for an airship to pick me up the next day. I couldn't leave town fast enough. I swore to myself that when I did finally go, it would be for the last time. There was nothing left for me in Rockville, not unless you counted the ghosts. I was through chasing ghosts.

Down in the tavern that night, I talked it all over with the bartender.

"I can't believe it either. What are the odds I just happen to pass her grave on my way out of that whole gargantuan cemetery? Hers was a newer looking grave. Couldn't have been more than five or ten years old, though hard to say for sure. There weren't any dates on it."

"A dateless grave? I never heard of such a thing."

"Me neither. I wonder what happened to her, and when."

"Well, whatever happened to her, it must have been more recent than five or ten years ago. Didn't you say she sent you a letter? Isn't that what brought you back to town in the first place? When did you say you got that letter again?"

The letter! I'd completely forgotten about it.

"That's right. She did send me a letter. How could she have sent me a letter, if she's dead?"

"Good question. The dead generally don't correspond via the postal service. Be a good goblin and fetch us that letter. Let's have a long look at it."

I brought the letter down from my room, un-crumpling it on the bar for examination. The bartender held it up to the candlelight, reading it aloud.

Dear Icarus,

I came over to your house today, but no one was home. I figured you'd be somewhere around the neighborhood, but you were nowhere around the neighborhood. I looked everywhere for you - up in the treehouse, down at the park, up and down Main Street. I saw your dad at the mine. He didn't know where you were either. I walked all the way across town through the woods to the river, thinking you might be fishing, or swimming. I walked far along the river, then farther, closer to the mountains. I went so far, I went and got myself lost in the summertime, without the time part. Are you lost too? If so, we should be lost together. Wouldn't that be fun?

THE IMAGINED HOMECOMING OF ICARUS ISAKOV

The rose is red
The violet blue
Dream a dream
Of me and you

Disrespectfully Yours,
Ruby Rockhollow

"Well, what do you make of it?"

"Are you sure it's her handwriting?"

"It's her handwriting. I'm sure." It was. I recognized it the moment I opened the letter, and the ruby red signature made it a certainty. She always used that color in her signature.

"You got the envelope?"

"No. I threw it away. There was no return address."

The bartender went on examining the letter silently. The bar wasn't busy, so he took his time. After a few minutes of studying it, he drew a strange conclusion.

"There is only one conclusion to conclude. This letter was sent to you from a dream. All this time you've been chasing memories, when you should have been chasing dreams."

"A *dream*? What dream?"

"Yes, a dream. *What dream* is the more difficult question. This doesn't read like any old daydream. Too nuanced. Definitely not an American dream. American one's aren't so interesting or mysterious. Could have been a midsummer night's dream. Hard to say for sure."

I had no idea what the bartender was talking about.

"The dreamcatcher - the one from the mine of secrets. Do you still have it?"

"I do."

"Good. I suspect you'll need it. I think that dreamcatcher is the pathway to the dream from which this letter was sent. The dreamcatcher was somehow left for you to find by Ruby, or by someone else, so that you could find her again. Case cracked. You're welcome."

Case cracked indeed. I'd found the dreamcatcher in the mine of secrets. If the bartender was right, I'd been mistaken in thinking the dreamcatcher was the secret to the castle. Instead, it was the secret to Ruby. Who'd left it for me there was a mystery, but I believed it had been left for me.

"How does the dreamcatcher work? Is it as easy as falling asleep with it hanging on my headboard?"

"It's not that simple. Where did you use to dream? And I don't mean in your bed. I mean where you imagined, wished, prayed, and played. Go there. Go to where you dreamed, when you used to dream. Go there with the dreamcatcher, and go to sleep."

I knew the place I dreamed when I used to dream. Ruby dreamed with me there. We passed countless hours there, laughing, playing, talking over those fantasies of childhood.

The place itself was a kind of fantasy. That's what treehouses are. They're forts of fantasy, meant for the exchange of secret dreams, among other things. Ruby's treehouse was no different.

Ruby's treehouse was where it always was, in her backyard. I saw it when I first arrived in town. I'd been shocked it was still intact. The rest of her house was a pile of rubble. I was less than enthusiastic about going back that way. My old neighborhood looked like a post-apocalyptic wasteland, and it was already getting dark out. There was also the fact Ruby was dead. I'd be going to the treehouse to find a dream, to find a dead girl. Sounds ridiculous even writing it. So, I decided it was a waste of time.

I resigned myself to an early, uneventful evening. I'd get a full night's sleep, and be on the way back to normalcy tomorrow. I said nothing to the bartender of my plans, but he must have sensed them. I left the bar, walking slowly and thoroughly defeated toward the stairs leading up to my room. When I reached the stairs, the bartender hollered at me.

"Icarus!"

"Yeah?"

"In the words of Aristotle, stop being such a candy-ass."

Those absurdist words of wisdom stopped me in my tracks. He was right, and I knew it. What harm was there in a visit to the old treehouse? I'd probably find nothing and no one, but at least I'd be certain Ruby was truly gone forever.

I hurried upstairs, grabbed the dreamcatcher from my room, then hurried back downstairs toward the front door of the Inn. I was on my way to the treehouse before you could say queen without a spleen.

***

I walked down an empty Main Street, under the glow of the pointless streetlights. Streetlights must be the last thing to go before a town croaks. Streetlights and bar lights. Above those lights, the sky had cleared of the gloom from earlier in the day. The stars were twinkling. The thinnest sickle of a moon smiled sideways like it knew something I didn't. A warm wind pushed me onward, down Main Street. It was shaping up to be a perfect summer night.

I turned off Main onto a side street that led into my old neighborhood. It was only eight o'clock, but you'd have guessed it the dead of night. My neighborhood was a black hole. There was no one anywhere. The only lights anywhere were from the fireflies. Legions of the blinking dots swarmed the empty streets. I wondered why there were so many. Maybe it was because there were no kids left to hunt and capture them —no natural predators.

I was almost at my old block when I passed a house with the lights on. The house fascinated me because it was the only house anywhere that showed any sign of life. It was a little stone cottage with a thatched roof. Looked like the oldest house in the universe. I never remembered it being there. I wondered who lived there and what they were doing.

My curiosity got the better of me, and I crept up to the living room window.

Inside was what looked like a replica of the living room from *Goodnight Moon*. On one side of the room, an old lady sat in a rocking chair, knitting. On the other side of the room, an old man sat in an armchair, fiddling with the knobs of an antique transistor radio. Between them, a small fireplace burned. Above the fire hung a faded, black and white picture of a much younger version of the couple.

The scene was what I'd expected, but as I stared inside, I felt something unexpected. For the first time since I'd arrived in the town, I felt hopeful for it. Rockville may have been declared dead by many (including me), but it never died for these two. And if it wasn't dead for someone, how could it be dead for anyone? There's a life after death for small towns. I could hear it through the static of the old transistor radio. It sounded like time.

Suddenly, I found myself staring straight into the wide eyes of an orange house cat. Without my noticing, the fat bastard had leaped onto the ledge on the opposite side of the window. The thing nearly gave me a heart attack. In my shock, I went flying backward over the bushes and onto the lawn. I scrambled up and jogged away down the block.

My block looked how it had when I'd visited earlier in the week. It was that same still life painting, only a much darker one. My old house looked seriously haunted, more so than before. Ruby's collapsed house looked equally infested with ghosts. Glad there was no need to go in either house. To the treehouse.

I walked down Ruby's driveway, which ran along the side of her house and into the backyard. There was once a detached garage back there, now gone except for the concrete foundation. Next to that was the big red oak tree, home to the treehouse. That tree was freakishly tall, easily one of the tallest in town. I'd always wondered if it might be older than the town itself, maybe the remnant of a once vast, now forgotten forest.

I waded through the uncut grass to the base of the tree and looked up. I could see the shadow of the treehouse way up there, where it always was. It was a simple treehouse, just a square wooden platform with wooden panels for walls. It was high in the tree, much higher than you'd expect a treehouse to be. I didn't remember it being so towering. It was like the treehouse grew higher with the tree itself over the years. I wondered how I'd climb up all that way in my grown-up state. Luckily, some climbing pegs were still nailed to the tree trunk.

I started up the pegs slowly, afraid they might come loose. They were miraculously sturdy. After the pegs, I had to work my way through another ten or so feet of branches. I'm no Spider-Man but managed it well enough. I was just below the base of the treehouse, breathing heavily, searching for the entrance –a square wooden board you pushed up to get inside– when I lost my footing. I'd have surely splattered to death below, had I not at the last second caught sight of a stray rope. What's a stray rope doing in a tree, you ask? A tire swing once dangled from the end of that rope. Just as I was slipping off my branch, I grabbed hold of it and climbed up into the treehouse.

I lay down a while up there, heart bulging, too tired and traumatized to move. After I settled down, I carefully stood up. I expected the treehouse to look much different than I remembered, but it hadn't changed at all. It looked the same as it always had, only a little smaller, because I was a little bigger. It seemed untouched like we'd only just played in it yesterday. There was our tree-stump table in the corner, surrounded by two pint-sized camping chairs. On the table were two cups of something we imagined, maybe a wizard's potion or witch's brew. A rotted checkerboard lay beside a rusty cap gun on the floor. Some old ornaments and wind chimes still dangled from the leafy ceiling above. I could see the tic-tack-toe we'd painted and played along the wooden walls. On one of the floorboards, I recognized a familiar carving. It read:

> *Great Scott*
> *Icarus Isakov is Piping Hot*

Ruby carved that and meant it in the literal sense. I'd once caught fire in the treehouse. It happened when we got the idea to smoke grass, long before we knew what *grass* really meant. Ruby rolled a construction paper joint, naturally packing it with freshly mowed front lawn grass. The grass happened to be quite dry. When I lit the "joint" and inhaled, it exploded into a ball of flames, tumbling straight into my lap, lighting half my shirt on fire. Ruby put the fire out with her own shirt, revealing her bra in the process, the first bra I ever saw.

I peeked over the edge of the treehouse, surprised at how high and hidden in the tree I was. No wonder the treehouse had remained undisturbed all these years. There was no one to see it or crazy enough to climb up. I looked down, over the rubble of Ruby's house, then at my own home. The back roof of my house was mostly caved in. Looking in through the roof, I could see the shadows of the tree branches and leaves dancing around my old bedroom.

I paced around the treehouse a long time, wondering, waiting for myself to get tired. I felt restless, but couldn't have climbed down from the treehouse if I wanted too. Climbing up was a near-death experience. Climbing down was suicide. The night was even darker than when I'd climbed up. There was no safe way to climb down, not without mangling myself. I'd have to wait until first light to climb down.

I took a bedtime piss over the side of the treehouse, then tied the dreamcatcher to a branch above, hopeful it would guide me to Ruby in the middle of the night. I lay down on my back, eyes finally blinking tiredly. The wind was blowing hard, and from every which way. I watched the branches swirl overhead and around the treehouse like the giant tentacles of some tree monster, screaming the sound of the rustling leaves, as though they were trying to tell me something. I didn't mind all that wind, because I was mostly sheltered from it. It rocked the treehouse back and forth, like a goblin cradle among the trees.

Before I knew it, I was fast asleep, dreaming this doozy of a dream.

Home

Before I'd even opened my eyes, I could tell I was somewhere else. I could tell from the smell. It was the unmistakable smell of freshly cut grass. It smelled like it always had, like summer, and not the summer of an abandoned mining town. Yards don't get cut in the summer of an abandoned mining town. The smell was that of a living, breathing, lawn-mowing Rockville.

I found myself still laying where I'd gone to sleep in the treehouse. The sun was already too high and shining too brightly. It looked to be mid-morning already, meaning I'd overslept. I rose in a panic. I had an airship to catch! Didn't I? I stood up, about to hurry down and out of the tree, when I noticed something strange. There was the decayed checkerboard, only now it looked brand new. It was sitting on the tree stump table, with the pieces perfectly set for a game. The two empty cups were now half-full of water. The cap gun was no longer rusty. It looked shiny and new, with fresh caps hanging from the back. I picked it up and pulled the trigger.

POP!

I looked out over the neighborhood. Ruby's backyard garage had magically reappeared. So had her whole house. I looked down toward my own home. The caved-in roof was no longer caved in. The broken windows were unbroken. The yard was all cleaned up. The house no longer looked haunted. It looked inhabited, how it had in its best days when I lived there. Looking in through my kitchen window, I could see someone moving around, cooking something.

MOM!

I maneuvered down through the branches, quick as a spider monkey. The tree seemed less tangled, and the treehouse less high. Hopping down into the grass, I found it no longer waist-high. It was inches high and freshly cut. Had I slept through a lawnmower? Impossible. And what was the tire swing doing back? I was in too much of a rush to solve those mysteries. I ran up Ruby's driveway, around her house, to the front door of my own.

The door was open. It was always open. I walked into the living room. It looked exactly how it always had. I walked past the broken fireplace, into the dining room. The dining room table was there, where it always was, with the very same soda stained tablecloth. The old liquor cabinet was there in the corner, looking not old at all. In the kitchen, I recognized the sound of my mom shuffling around. She also recognized the sound of me.

"Icarus? I'm making *cooooooooookies*." Mom's voice, unmistakable as the freshly cut grass.

I floated into our little galley kitchen, in a sort of trance. I was overwhelmed with disbelief, then delight, at the scent of cookie dough and the sight of my mom. She turned to me with a smile so big it just missed crushing me to death. She looked like a culinary goddess in that polka dot apron, and I'm not just saying that. My mom was the most beautiful mom in all of Rockville. It was an absolute fact. She looked like the state of grace just stirring cookie dough.

"Here, try some."

I hugged her instead.

"What's gotten into you?" She giggled, hugging me back. "Try some dough."

She held the cookie-dough drenched spatula up to my mouth. I licked it clean as a dragon's tooth. The dough tasted sweet as it always had, how it had at the Inn, that first night I returned to town. As I licked another spatula clean, I heard an open and closing of the front door.

"Oh, your father must be home early."

I smelled him before I saw him. That musty, dusty scent of the mine followed him wherever he went. I rushed out of the kitchen through the dining room. Turning the corner into the living room, I ran squarely into his wide, filthy chest. He'd heard me and was waiting in ambush. He picked me up and bear-hugged me until I couldn't stand it, until my eyes nearly bugged out of my head - a customary ritual after he'd finished work. He looked in his prime, all rangy and muscly, with that big bushy blue beard.

"Punched out early today. Too damned nice aboveground to spend the day underground. What devilry is your mother concocting in the kitchen? Smells sweet as skilamalink!"

I followed him into the kitchen, where he surprised mom from behind.

"Ahhh! Unhand me! The cookie dough is over there. No, over there. Mind the stove!"

Dad and I proceeded to devour the dough, but only for a few seconds. We were chased out of the kitchen by a frying pan wielding mom. We were herded out the back door and into the backyard. Dad made his way to the garden. He was obsessed with his garden, and he wasn't even a good gardener. I watched him wander through the garden from the back porch, wondering why he wasn't more interested in me.

My parents acted as if it were an ordinary day, as if they'd just seen me yesterday, as if they were still alive. I instinctively played along, though I wasn't quite sure of the game. I wondered if I might be in a dream, but couldn't be sure. The thing about dreaming is, while you're doing the dreaming, you'd never in a million years guess yourself to be dreaming. The realization tends to happen only when you wake up.

The day was strange. At times, everything seemed more real than real. At other times, there were hints of the surreal. Parts of things were fringed with fantasy. The sun sometimes disappeared, blending in with the rest of the sky, changing its shade from blue to blonde. The leaves on certain trees were all in black and white. The front porch flowers looked like cartoons, like they'd been drawn into the scene. The glass windows in Ruby's house had turned to stained glass, making the place look like a little lost church.

There were times I felt like I was hallucinating. I wondered what new reality I was in, and how I'd gotten there. Was I, in fact, dreaming? Had I gone time traveling in the middle of the night in a treehouse time machine? Maybe I'd fallen from the tree into a wormhole, and entered an alternative universe. Was I dead? Was this heaven? It felt like it, so far at least.

I hung around the house a while, crowding my mom in the kitchen, eating, talking, indulging myself in the past turned present. I'd have never left, had it not been for Ruby. I figured if my parents were back, maybe Ruby was also. I walked over to her house to see if she was home.

Her front door was shut, guarded by the same big brass boar door knocker. The boar looked somehow different. When I reached out to knock it, it moved. First, it only growled at me, but when I reached closer, it snapped at me. Nearly skewered a finger. I avoided the surly knocker, knocking on the window instead. No answer. I knocked a few more times on the front door, then went around back and knocked a few more knocks there. No one was home.

When I went back to my house, I found it just as empty

as Ruby's. My parents had disappeared without a trace. The front door was open, so I searched the house up and down. Everything in the house was unchanged, but my parents were nowhere to be found. I wondered how that could be. I'd only been gone a few minutes. Wherever they'd gone, I got the feeling they weren't coming back, and that it was time for me to do the same.

***

I made my way downtown, walking back down my block, the same way I'd come the night before. The neighborhood looked totally different. The houses looked mended and tended. Cars lined the streets. There were townsfolk everywhere. I saw kids playing tag, dads trimming hedges, and moms watering flowers. Rockville was reborn overnight.

Walking through the neighborhood, I saw all those houses and families I'd once known. The Steelman's had emerged from the jungle of overgrowth that suffocated it. Don Steelman, oldest of the Steelman boys, waxed his red corvette out front. That corvette was a fixture in the Steelman driveway. Never ran. Just sat there, beaming for all to behold. The Silverfox's place was so full of kids they were falling out of the goddamned windows. Mrs. Silverfox watered the lawn with a smile on her face, waving to me as I passed by like it was any other day. The Pinkmoon place still looked run down, just less run down. The Hopleaf house had been rebuilt overnight from the nothing it was. That wrap around porch was the envy of the neighborhood. Mr. Hopleaf sat on the front porch swing, reading the newspaper, smoking from that gargantuan corncob pipe the way he always did. The Rockhold house returned. My old pal Robin Rockhold was out front mowing the lawn. He stopped mowing when he saw me.

"Hey Icarus! I'm on the clock all morning, but let's have a coke later?"

Coke was code for smoke. Robin started smoking shortly after he was potty-trained.

"Yeah Robin, yeah cokes later. See ya then." I waved goodbye as I turned down Main Street.

Main Street looked like it had dropped acid. The cars zooming down it left tracers in their wake, like the ones you see in long exposure photography. The tracers were so long and unbroken I could hardly see the breaks between cars. I wondered how I'd ever cross the street.

I walked on and into downtown. The night before, all that was open for business were the streetlights. Now, everything was. A crowd of old goblins gathered around the Main Theatre for a matinee. A bunch of young goblins sat on the curb outside the Corner Candy Shop, inhaling globs of rainbow. The boards had disappeared from the front of the old, nameless diner. Looking in its windows, I saw all the coffee-drinkers, cake-eaters, and tip-takers. These were the people, and this was the town that I came back for. For the first time since I'd returned home, I felt at home.

I walked into the Rexall corner drug store for a soda. The drug store was one of the few businesses still open when I'd first returned to town. The inside looked pretty much the same, albeit cleaner and busier. I walked through to the back of the store, to the old-fashioned soda fountain bar. There were a couple of others sitting at the bar, already sipping from colorful bottles. I ahemmed the soda bartender, who had his back to me. When he turned around, I recognized him. The soda bartender was my very same faun bartender from the Forgetful Faun Inn.

"Why, if it isn't Icarus Isakov. Fine day, wouldn't you say? Or is night? Ha! You look surprised. Don't be. Didn't I tell you, I moonlight as a oneironaut? That means dream navigator." He was dressed up for the dream, wearing an old-fashioned barman tuxedo. "Any-hoo, what can I get ya? I recommend something straight from the soda fountain. I'm telling you, this fountain tastes like the fountain of youth."

"What are you doing here? And where, while we're on the subject, is *here*?"

"I'm doing what I'm always doing, tending the bar. I just happen to be serving unusual soda's, instead of the usual memories." He served me a soda from the fountain. "There are no memories here, because *here* is a dream, and dreams don't remember."

"So, I am dreaming then? Figured as much."

"Not exactly. You're dreaming, but this isn't your dream. This is the town's dream."

"The town's dream? Towns don't dream."

"Towns *do* dream. A town has a life, just like you and me, only a more collective and complex one. A town has its own style, habits, and thoughts. Towns have souls, even small towns, like this one. Find me a soul, and I'll find you a dream for it."

"Am I awake then? Awake in the town's dream?"

"No. You're dreaming alright. It's just not your dream."

So, I was in a dream, the first-ever dream I dreamed that wasn't mine, as far as I know. The dreaming would explain the fantastical features of the day. Just then, I noticed my soda mug was glowing and oozing like a lava lamp. Apart from strange sights like that, I didn't feel like I was dreaming. I felt fully conscious and in control of myself. I drank soda and talked to the bartender and may as well have been wide awake.

"Is Ruby here?"

"What would a dream be without the girl of your dreams? Last I heard, your Ruby is a princess here. Last I checked, princesses live in castles..."

I downed my dream soda, then turned toward the door. Next stop, the castle.

"Before you go, remember what I said, about remembering? Dreams don't remember. Nor do they keep time. Ruby will recognize you, but she won't remember you, if you get my meaning. Small town dreams survive their towns because they don't grow old."

I thanked the dream drifting bartender and made my way out of the drug store to the edge of town, to the castle. It was a short walk. From a distance, I could see storm clouds gathering over and around it. Upon closer examination, I found the castle itself looking much different than it had when I'd visited it during the week. It looked occupied and unwelcoming.

As I walked up, the castle creatures scurried to the ramparts and gatehouse towers facing my road leading up to the front gate. They were expecting me. There were gorgons, demogorgons, demons, dragons, dark goblins, and every other sort of monster. I even spotted a lawyer somewhere in there. They cackled and jeered at me with distorted faces and empty eyes. Here was what looked to be more nightmare than a dream. Not what I expected. Not what I expected at all.

The castle gatehouse, where I'd once thought the Watchman kept watch, was still there. The dark pathway leading inside the castle was inaccessible, closed off by the portcullis. I stood there awhile, getting threatened and laughed at, wondering what to do, until I heard that familiar sound, that roller-coaster clicking sound.

Clickety-click, click, click...

The portcullis was opening, ever so slowly. The last time it opened, I'd expected the Watchman. Instead, I'd gotten a gnome. I wouldn't be so lucky this time. I knew it. I watched, as from the shadows under the archway emerged another shadow.

The Watchman.

I'd say the whole of him was four, maybe five times my size. His torso alone looked about three times my size, more than heavy enough to crush me to death. The spiked mace he carried was easily twice my size, also more than heavy enough to crush me to death. The shield he had was closer to my own goblin dimensions, but probably just heavy enough to crush me to death. Point being, I was outsized and on the verge of being crushed to death.

As the Watchman came closer, I saw he was draped in a cloak, and no ordinary garment. It was one of those mystical cloaks, stitched with small-town nightmares. The nightmares moved as he moved, making it seem like he was standing in front of a movie projector. I saw a ruby-less ruby mine, surrounded by crowds of starved miners marching across his shoulders like a defeated army. Graves polka-dotted one arm, his other arm looked like Skid Row. Whole neighborhoods of houses crumbled down his chest into the river that ran across his waist like a belt. Below the river, mountains collapsed into Main Street. Fast-ticking, grimacing clock faces lined the bottom trim of the cloak as if to say the town's time had come. It had. Now my time was come.

The moment he stopped in front of me, the dream stilled. The jeering from the castle quieted. The wind faded. The color drained from the sky. The Watchman wore what looked like a gladiator's helmet, with a black horsetail crest like a mohawk across the top. Under the helmet was the faceless shadow of the Watchman, watching me.

I stood staring at where I guessed his eyes might be. Instead of smashing me to smithereens, he stared back, then laughed. It was a laughter so long and deep it shook the ground, and you'd have thought it came from the depths of the mine, underneath the town. Once he finished laughing, he raised his mace and started toward me.

Just then, I noticed there was a sword in my hand. I had no idea how the sword got there, but there it was, clearly put there by someone who intended for me to use it. It was a scimitar with a thick, curved blade, perfect for slashing. Grabbing hold of it, I regained my confidence. I was a white goblin knight on his way to rescue a captive princess. I was unstoppable, invincible. Ferocious. The Watchman's watching days were over.

The Watchman charged at me as the whole castle garrison cheered him on. He swung the mace at me with a wide, sweeping stroke that I saw coming from a mile away. I ducked it and slashed him good behind the kneecaps as he went hurling by me. The castle fell silent. The Watchman stopped, feeling the back of his knee, but only for a second. He stood up, turned around, and laughed that deep laugh again. The slash had no effect.

He charged again, this time holding the mace high above his head. I tried the same duck and slash maneuver, but he was ready for it. He stopped just short of me, causing me to lose my balance and fall forward onto my hands and knees. He then smashed the mace into my exposed back with the force of a meteor. It really did feel like a meteor. It felt like I'd been smashed straight through the crust of the earth. My body was split into at least three pieces, maybe four.

I wasn't in any pain, but I knew I was dead. All I could feel was the pressure from the Watchman's mace, hammering my body into oblivion, thrashing it over and over and over again. I could hear my bones cracking, breaking, being ground to dust. Between blows, I could hear the echoes of laughter from the castle walls. I looked up with my one remaining eyeball and saw the Watchman's boot come down and squash it like a pea.

I was defeated. No, demolished. As I lay there, shattered into little goblin bits, I reflected on the shattered dream. Who was I kidding? I was no hero. There was no one to even save. Ruby was long gone. So was Rockville. So was I. I was defeated, done, dead. This was no dream; it was a nightmare. I was beaten to death by a nightmare.

Or was I?

Can you declare yourself dead after you're already dead? Can you complain about it afterward? No. Yet, I was undoubtedly complaining. I realized then that I wasn't dead, and the dream wasn't over. The thing about nightmares is, they can't kill you.

This occurred to me as I lay there, getting pounded and

grounded to bone meal. I realized I was still fully conscious when I should have been unconscious. Not only was I conscious, I felt better. I was hopeless no more. The moment I had my nightmare epiphany, I felt whole again, and I was. I found myself standing in front of the castle, in front of the Watchman.

Ding Dong rang the round two bell. It would be a quick round.

Surest way to conquer a nightmare is to dream yourself a Colt .45 single action revolver. You may think me dishonorable for using such an unfair weapon, but all is fair in love and war. As soon as I had taken shape again, I blew a hole in the Watchman's chest the size of Siberia.

The Watchmen spontaneously combusted in an explosion of light and color. The bright, shining fragments splattered up into the sky and all over the castle, transforming it from a castle of nightmares to one of dreams. You'd have thought I'd killed the Devil himself, the way all his fiendish friends vaporized, replaced with flowers and fairies and all that. The storm clouds cleared, letting down the sunlight, changing the color of the whole castle from iron to ivory.

The castle was suddenly approachable, so I approached.

***

I passed underneath the archway of the gatehouse into

167

the courtyard. It was the same courtyard, with those finely trimmed, bright green hedges, and those colorful flowers lining the red brick walkways. When I'd first visited it, in my waking state, the courtyard was completely empty of anyone. Now, it was full. The castle-goers cheered the moment I emerged victorious from the gatehouse. I was the humbled hero of the day, conquering champion of the Watchman. I stood there stunned awhile, giving my best royal wave, shaking hands, hugging hugs, feeling famously famous.

Eventually, I made my way through the crowded courtyard to the castle keep. I guessed if a princess was anywhere, it would be there, with the rest of the royal court. The keep looked different, more massive and mysterious than it had when I'd first visited. It still looked like a medieval cathedral, but the edges were all curved and in some places distorted. The color of the stone was swirled and smeared in certain places like a Van Gogh painting come to life.

The inside of the castle looked so different; it was like I'd never been there. It was fully furnished and occupied, how I'd expected it to be when I'd first visited. There were coats of arms, suits of armor, red carpets, magic carpets, tapestries, fireplaces on fire, tapestries of fireplaces on fire, and people. Lots of people. There were courtiers, cooks, falconers, cellerers, chanceries, knights, even the odd ghost. The great hall was so greatly busy that no one took notice of me as I walked in. No one that is, except for the girl who sat on the throne at the far end of the great hall.

Ruby.

I walked nervously down the long hall toward her, wondering what the proper etiquette was when reintroducing yourself to the girl next door, turned princess. Should I bow? Kneel? Was it still Ruby, or was it her highness? Was I to be knighted? What would I say to her? What would she say to me? As all these questions raced through my head, my shadow shone beside me in an impossible technicolor, reminding me it was all just a dream. That helped me relax some.

Ruby looked how I remembered her. She wasn't dressed like a princess. She was dressed like the girl she was, the girl with a handful of dresses to her name. She wore a faded white summer dress. It hung loose and long on her, all the way down to her moccasins. On her head was a crown of wildflowers she often wore. She sat upon a ridiculously oversized throne, dangling her feet playfully. In the strange castle light, her age was hard to say. One second she was a woman, the next a little girl, then a woman again. She finally settled somewhere in between, somewhere much younger than me, younger than was possible for her to be.

"Icarus?" She looked at me wide-eyed, as if she wasn't sure it was really me.

I wanted to scream HELLO! Been forever, hasn't it? I never dreamed I'd see you again, yet here I am, dreaming you again. Your hair, it looks longer, lighter than I

169

remember. I like it. No, I really do. Lovely flowers, by the way. They look puritanical. Ha! Just kidding, just kidding. You look wild. Wild as wildflowers. Me? I'm fine, growing more uninteresting by the day. Live in the city. Work hard play hard you know that sort of shtick. How are you? Where are you? Where are we?

Thankfully, I said none of that. There was so much I wanted to say I couldn't say any of it. The thoughts got all tangled and mangled in her hair before I could get them out.

"Icarus, what's *happened* to you? You look like you work in a bank."

What had happened to me? I felt like Wendy Darling, when Peter returns from Neverland, sees she's all grown up, and is thoroughly disgusted by the whole matter. I remembered what the bartender said, how dreams don't remember, how time doesn't pass in them. Ruby was expecting the Icarus Isakov from long ago. I felt like I'd betrayed her.

"My apologies, your highness."

"How did it happen, this growing up of yours?"

How *did* it happen, I wondered? Not when I turned eighteen. Not even close. Was it when I graduated from college? No. It was later than that. I found it hard to pinpoint the exact moment it happened. All I knew for sure was that it happened sometime after I left Rockville.

"I caught growing up like a cold, from the city. Had I stayed here in town, I'd surely have not caught it at all. I have no excuse for it. I'm ashamed, your grace."

I bowed my head, wondering if she'd order for it to be cut off.

"Very well. You've atoned for the growing up by vanquishing the Watchman, I suppose. He was the most watchful Watchman. He had me convinced the ruby mine ran out of rubies! Can you believe that?"

We laughed awkwardly at each other, then stared awkwardly at each other over the awkward chasm of time and memory between us. All you can do to bridge the divide in those situations is small talk. So, we did. She started.

"You aren't rich, are you? I find there is a strong correlation between assholery and assets."

"No, not remotely rich, your excellency. Hardly upper middle class."

"That's very well. Keep it that way, and we can be friends, again."

"As you wish, your majesty."

"Call me Ruby."

Ruby leapt down from the throne in a whirl of white dress.

She was done playing at princess. It was time for a new game, one with me. She took me by the hand, leading me sprinting down the long castle hall. I was barely able to keep up with her. If I wasn't dreaming, I'm sure I'd have torn a hamstring. I hardly even noticed my legs were still attached to my body. Who notices their legs in dreams? Not you. Not me. Not anyone. The castle-goers noticed, though. They all stopped to stare as we raced by. We ran straight through the doors of the keep, back into the courtyard.

Only the courtyard was gone. A full-blown carnival had somehow replaced it during the short time I'd been inside the keep. The carnival looked empty, yet fully alight and operational. Ruby led me to an entrance at the base of the keep stairs, where I half expected a carny to ask me for my ticket. There was no carny to be found, anywhere. There wasn't anyone to be found anywhere. The lights were lit and the rides rode without anyone operating them.

We wandered through the carnival, hand in hand, stopping here or there for this or that. We played games. We played skeeball and popa-shot. I won her a giant, stuffed gogmagog in the ring toss. We mainlined sugar. We ate elephant ears and cotton candy served by no one, yet there for anyone. We rode rides. We defied gravity on the gravitron, scrambled our brains on the scrambler, and bumped ourselves to whiplash on the bumper cars. With the park opened to us, but closed to everyone else, there was no waiting for anything. It was magnificent.

The carnival was like old times. So much so, it seemed like we'd done it a time or two before. Maybe we had. The carnival wasn't all that different from the midsummer one we went to every year as kids. Only thing missing was kids. The little monsters running wild with black cats and bottle rockets. The fairies chasing goblins with sparklers. The goblins chasing fairies with bang snaps. The dads drinking Budweiser. The moms smoking Newports. All the cut-off jeans. They were all gone. It was just me and Ruby. I think that was how she intended it.

We spent the rest of the dream's afternoon playing in the courtyard carnival. The sun was ducking behind the mountains when Ruby asked me to ride just one more ride. I was surprised at that, because I was sure we'd rode every ride, twice. She led me out of the castle, down a hill nearer to the mountains, into some woods.

We weren't far into the woods when I saw something that didn't belong in the woods. It was an electric glow, coming from a meadow up ahead. In that meadow, we came upon a forgotten Ferris wheel. It looked like my own Ferris wheel dreamcatcher, come to life. It sat strangely alone and out of place, spinning over a narrow stretch of the river that was somehow flecked with the red and yellow spots of autumn leaves, despite it being summer.

I stared at the Ferris wheel. Ruby stared at me.

"What do you intend to do? Will you ask me to ride the Ferris wheel, or will you ask the Ferris wheel to ride me?"

"Yes," was all I could think to say.

The Ferris wheel stopped on cue as we approached like it saw us coming. The moment we sat down next to each other in the carriage, it jerked forward into motion, spinning as slowly as you'd expect any Ferris wheel to turn. We circled pleasantly around, talking, making up for lost time, rocking gently in the wind. We dipped down into the darkening woods, then up into the brighter twilight, the river rustling below us. It was an unspectacular ride, but that soon changed. It changed when the Ferris wheel started flying.

I hardly noticed it, at first. The Ferris wheel must have come off its axle at some point. Instead of tumbling to the ground, as you'd expect it to, it went spinning on forward in defiance of gravity, like a runaway racecar tire come off by accident. We spun slowly forward to the end of the meadow. Just before crashing into the woods, our trajectory changed, and we took off over the trees, soaring into the night sky, toward town.

It was fine up there, Ferris-wheeling through the night air. We drifted higher and higher over the town like a couple of regular Mary Poppins's. Looking down, I could see the whole of Rockville, as it once was. The church caught my eye first, being the tallest building in town. The lights were on in the sanctuary. Probably Priest O'Hagan binging a fresh batch of the sacrament. Next door was the blinking marquee of the roller-rink. Kids lined up around the block, waiting to get in. Sparks of red fire and ruby shone from the still operating mine. Miners lined up around the outside, waiting to punch out. I saw the lights and heard the whistle of an approaching freight train. It passed by the pool, which looked to be open late. Night swimming, I presume. The street lights flickered on all at once, illuminating all the dots of townsfolk lining the sidewalks. On my old block were the faster moving dots of kids at play. Headlights lit up Main Street like an electric river. The actual river was darker. I could see the shape of it, slithering around town, the boundary separating Rockville from the wide world beyond.

Once we'd drifted to the outskirts of town, the Ferris wheel turned slowly around, heading back the way we'd come, back toward the mountains. I guessed we'd be landing in the same spot we'd taken off from, but we passed right over it. Landing wasn't part of the plan. We flew higher and higher, instead of lower and lower. The chatter of the town faded away, replaced by the whispering pines of the mountain. They whispered what sounded like secrets.

Above us, the night was coming to life. One of those fluffy, cotton candy moons rose from behind the mountains, joining the strangest stars. The stars were odd because they were all in motion. There were whole constellations dancing above us, with enough starry spirits to fill an interstellar zoo. There were jeweled serpents, scorpions, jinns, jackalopes, hippocamps, and heroes. A sparkling giant skipped asteroids through the milk of the Milky Way. A flock of twinkles twirled and whirled in synchronized orbit. A pegasus of comets blazed under us at about a thousand miles per hour, right through the spokes of the Ferris wheel. That left the whole Ferris wheel shaking something awful. Once it stopped shaking, it stopped spinning.

I looked for Ruby, but she was gone, from the Ferris wheel, at least. I saw her not far away, walking through the night sky like it was nothing special, like she was out for a stroll down Main Street. That long white dress of hers was blowing so wildly in the wind I thought she might blow away altogether. But she didn't blow away. She danced. She danced a private dance for me. It'll be hard to write that dance justice, but I'll try.

She danced this sort of space-aged square dance. First, she hiked her dress up, tapping those old moccasins on the invisible dance floor. The strange thing about that tap was *how* it tapped. It struck like not so faraway thunder every time she tapped it. The thunder rumbled on even after she was done tapping, as she do-si-doed around the stars like they were dance partners. The stars were aware of her, growing fuller and larger, moving toward her and with her, twirling in and around her like the whole thing was choreographed. She danced close by me, smiling an invite to come out and join her for a promenade, but I was too chicken shit to get out of the Ferris wheel. She spun slowly away from me, sashaying with the man on the moon instead. When the lightning started, she started moving, and I mean *really moving*. She was twisting and turning, hooting and hollering all through the atmosphere like a flying, hillbilly contortionist.

She stopped dancing when the rain started. It came down slowly at first. Ruby held her palms out and up, catching the first drops like a surprised little kid. I signaled for her to come back in the Ferris wheel carriage, where she'd be sheltered from the rain, but she didn't. She had no intention of ever coming back in the Ferris wheel. I could tell it from the way she smiled at me.

Then it started pouring. I'm talking mythological deluge. And there was something strange about that rain. It was gradually blurring everything around me, and not just because it was coming down so hard and heavy. That rain came down like the silver strokes of some cosmological paintbrush, painting over the whole world. The town below had already completely disappeared, as had the castle and mountains. I looked down and around, where I saw the Ferris wheel itself being washed away. Ruby stood out in the rain, fading away herself.

I realized then that the dream was at an end, that something must be done.

I gathered up the courage to step out of the Ferris wheel into the sky. I hadn't noticed it until then, but I was completely weightless. I walked on the sky just fine, just like Ruby. The rain fell harder and faster than ever as I rushed toward her. By the time I reached her, most everything was gone, except us.

There, at the end of it all, Ruby appeared older, I guess the oldest she ever got. She was a woman, but no less beautiful than she ever was as a girl. Despite the rain, she was dry as a bone. She smiled at me and said something, but the words drowned out in the rain. Everything was quickly becoming dim and distorted, which made me feel like the highest goblin in the galaxy. Ruby looked imaginary. I reached out, wiping the orange freckles from her face like specks of clay. Her eyes gleamed, but I couldn't decide on their color. They changed like a stoplight. Red. Yellow. Orange. Blue. Green. Red again. Her hair curled and uncurled before my eyes, falling straight down to her shoulders before bouncing back up again. The crown of flowers shone from her head like a halo, making her look like an angel from a nursery rhyme.

Then, she kissed me. I'm sorry to say it wasn't a lusty, magical kiss of the sort that cures cancer or raises the dead. You should know by now, I'm no prince. As for Ruby, she may have been a princess, but only in dreams. No, that kiss was not of the fairytale sort. It was a goodbye kiss, given to me by the girl next door, gone away forever. We may have been dreaming, but that kiss tasted like the real thing. It tasted like one of those mysterious flavors of childhood, like the blue in blue moon ice cream, or the pink in pink lemonade.

It tasted like Ruby. Like home.

Forgettery

I woke up in the treehouse, in the same place I'd fallen asleep the night before. For a second, I thought I was still in the Ferris wheel carriage. The treehouse was about the same size as the carriage. But the flying Ferris wheel was gone, transformed back to its flightless, dreamcatcher dimensions. I saw it, dangling from the tree branch I'd hung it on the night before.

Looking around, I saw everything was as it was from the night before. The treehouse boards were rotted. The treehouse toys were aged. The backyard below was once again an overgrown wilderness. No freshly cut grass. No scent of newly mown grass. Not a sound in town. My house was empty again. Ruby's house was gone, along with Ruby. Along with everything else.

I somehow climbed down from the treehouse without mangling myself. I felt less spry than when I'd been weightlessly dreaming. On top of that, I was tight as a clam from having slept on a slab of wood. Once I made it down, I started back toward the Inn. I had a flight to catch.

It was a bleak and windy day, the first hints of autumn

in the air. I found the neighborhood deserted again. It seemed a different place from the dream altogether. The dream wasn't one of those elusive ones, forgotten the moment you wake. It was the opposite. I remembered all of it. Still remember it today. I expect it'll be one of the last things I ever forget.

Walking back, I felt all the feels. I was happy at having finally found Ruby, but sad at the final goodbye. I was hopeful to move on from the town, but hopeless for its future. More than anything, I felt a sense of wonder at the trip. The Forgetful Faun Inn, proudly serving the past, where tomorrow is not welcome today. The Lighthouse of the Lost, where I was ass-kicked from the highest height by a lighthouse-keeping cat into the waters of the wishing well. The mermaid who saved me from that sea of wishes. The mine of secrets, where the last miner led me to the deepest, darkest of secrets, and to the dreamcatcher. The dreamcatcher, catching me a dream with Ruby, in our treehouse. The dream of the past. The dream where dreams come true.

Back at the Inn, I prepared to leave in a hurry. The airship was scheduled to pick me up around mid-day, and it was already mid-morning. Once I'd packed, I made my way downstairs to the bar. I planned to grab a quick meal and to say farewell to the bartender.

The bar was empty, except for the bartender. I thanked him with a tip, which he refused. He thanked me back with a brunch, which I accepted. As I ate, it dawned on me I'd never asked the bartender his name. That struck me, and probably you too, as a preposterous oversight. I asked him his name, and apologized for not having asked it sooner.

"My name? I figured it went without saying. It's on the sign outside, after all. I'm the one and only Forgetful Faun."

"Oh. Of, of course, you are..." I babbled, sounding and feeling dense. "Strange name for someone specializing in the business of remembering." Which it was.

"Who says I'm not also in the business of forgetting? Who says I can't serve a drink to forget? You look like you could use some forgetting. Allow me to fix you up a forgettery."

He whipped me up a bubbly concoction, green as leprechaun piss, served in a tulip glass.

"I call this one the piper at the gates of dawn. Try it, if you dare forget."

"What will it make me forget, exactly?" Fair question, I thought. If I could selectively forget, I might need a larger glass of this stuff.

"What *won't* it allow you to forget is the better question. Drink that, and you'll forget all that's worth forgetting. You'll forget all the lost souls you've lost, all the times you can't have back, all the times you don't want back, every rejection, dejection, dissatisfaction, every last bit of the sad past lingering in that goblin noggin. That drink will unbreak your heart, fast as you swallow it. That drink is deliverance, from the past."

I looked at the fizzy, forgetful cocktail, wondering at the consequences of my drinking it, of forgetting. I wondered if the past was doing me any favors. Everyone says growing up is the hard part, but I don't think so. I think it's the growing down that's hardest. And it's not the getting old, it's the realization we were once young. It's the remembering that makes it so difficult. I was happiest as a kid before I hardly had a past to remember, before the unsorted baggage of years crowded my skull. If only I could forget the past, could I be that same careless kid?

I picked up the drink and took a whiff. It smelled careless, with a hint of lime. Highly drinkable. Here goes nothing. I had the drink to my lips when the bartender interrupted my forgetting.

"There *is* something to be said about remembering. Stories, even the made-up sort, they're born from memory. You can't have stories without memories. Well, no good ones at least. Take your own story. Yeah, it might be sad in parts, but you can't have happily ever after from start to finish. That would make for the worst story of all time."

I put the drink down, second thoughts being thought.

"Now me, I don't have a story. Not a single page. I've been drinking forgetteries since I don't remember when. Some days, I'm lucky if I remember to wipe my ass. The best I'll ever be is a character in someone else's story. Granted, that's how I intended it. Don't remember when I intended it, but I must have. Anyway, before you sip that drink, make sure the whole of your story, from start to finish, has more worth forgetting than remembering."

I pushed the drink away from me, my mood changed. I was still thirsty, but for something else.

"Make it a memory, instead."

The bartender served me my last memory of the trip. It was one worth remembering. They all were. Remembering is not the problem. Forgetting is. That's why I'd stayed away from Rockville for so long. I'd forgotten, or been trying to forget, my own story. But that story was inseparable from home. The past is as much a part of me as my horns. No use fighting, forgetting it. If I were to forget, I'd have forgotten my whole goblin self in the process.

***

The airship picked me up where it dropped me off, where Main Street loses its name and turns to gravel on the edge of town. I walked there, down the middle of the empty street, through the middle of the empty town. Of course, there was no one to see me off, no one to say goodbye to. Fine by me. I always preferred an Irish goodbye to the real thing. Less dramatic.

The ship was waiting for me. It was the same rickety contraption I'd flown in on. There were a handful of other passengers already onboard, mostly goblins. They looked like me, like escapees from other small towns. The same geriatric, half-blind captain commandeered the vessel.

Wonderful. He recognized me, squinting at me with his good eye as I boarded.

"Welcome back sonny! How was Nowheresville?"

"Just how I remembered it."

We took a wide, slow berth around the town as the captain steered the airship back toward the city. I looked over the side of the deck, down at the town below. It looked much different than it had from the Ferris wheel. I could see the streets and downtown, but that was about it. The individual houses were so covered in overgrowth I could hardly distinguish them from the surrounding fields. Rockville looked more ancient ruins than modern town. That made sense to me because there's a mythology we associate with ancient ruins. Mythology is the fantasy we use to make sense of the world. That's what Rockville had become for me. Mythology.

I think that's what home becomes for all of us, eventually.

An Unexpected Letter

The rest of that summer was short. Autumn was even shorter. Some said summer skipped it altogether, speeding straight on through it to winter. Sure felt that way. One day, I was beaching in a t-shirt and shorts, the next I was hunched over a fireplace, draped in the old Chesterfield. I don't mind wrapping myself in the old Chesterfield, but I prefer to do so in the winter season. The skipping of autumn made for the longest, coldest stretch in city history.

When winter was at its worst, I hosted a modest soiree at my apartment. I got the idea to thaw everyone's frozen spirits with actual spirits, and a hot, home-cooked meal. I spared no expense for the gathering. There was the finest in boxed wine, sophisticated starters, streaming synthwave, even non-plastic silverware was provided to the dozen or so lucky guests. I served a sneakily succulent dinner of Cockaigne cockatrice and deviled whelp eggs. Sneakily succulent! I swear to you, someone at the dinner called it that. I felt like a goblin Gordon Ramsay.

Everyone squeezed around my little dining room table, where we ate, drank, and talked. We told stories of the past worth telling. We guessed at stories of the future yet to be told. There were debates between the debaters. Jokes between the jokers. Someone complained about the Catholic Church. Someone else complained about taxes. Those two subjects led to a debate on the tax exempted status of the Catholic Church and jokes about priests.

The snow arrived uninvited, just after dinner. We were all surprised by the amount of it, dumping down in great white doughy gobs. There was hardly more than a sprinkle in the forecast. No one would be leaving, not anytime soon. The snow was falling too hard and looked too beautiful from the inside.

So, I suggested a game.

I cleared the dinner table and placed a small glass of salamander brandy in the center. You might not believe in goblins or fairies, but salamander brandy is a real thing. Look it up. It's a hallucinogenic spirit, like absinthe, only stronger. It tastes worse than it sounds. Far worse. It's made by hanging a slimy salamander upside down under a flow of brandy during distillation. The salamander excretes poisons to defend itself, blending with the brandy. The resulting concoction is an amphibian-tasting, psychoactive mud, meant to be avoided at all costs.

The game was played by placing marbles in a hat, one for each player. All the marbles were white, except one, which was red. Players pass the hat around, pulling one marble from the hat at a time. The first player to pull out the red marble loses, being forced to drink the entire glass of salamander brandy. It's a simple game of chance, but with high stakes.

The game started, everyone passing the marble-filled hat around the table excitedly. Because I'd strategically positioned myself as one of the last to pick from the hat, I liked my odds. Still, I watched nervously as the game unfolded. Here we go.

White marble.

White marble.

My odds were worsening by the second.

White marble.

White marble.

Shit.

White marble.

Who suggested this game again?

White marble. White marble. White marble.

Someone pick the fucking red marble!

White marble.

My turn...

Red marble.

The table exploded in laughter. My loss was a victory for everyone else who'd been spared the salamander brandy. I put on a fake smile, wondering why I hadn't suggested a game of Jenga. Everyone loves Jenga. Too late now. Someone turned down the stereo for dramatic effect. Someone else handed me the skunky glass. Everyone stared at me, waiting.

I bravely downed the glass. Barely. It tasted more like salamander than brandy. It tasted like poison. Getting the drink down was an ordeal, keeping it down was nearly impossible. The gooeyness of it caused the crappiest essence to linger in my mouth and throat. I rushed to the bathroom, where I dry-heaved and dry-heaved, to the crying laughter of everyone else. I somehow kept it down, but the damage was done.

I stumbled into the living room, sprawling onto my couch. I was surprised at how quickly the hallucinations started. Looking outside my window at the falling snow, I saw the snowflakes weren't snowflakes at all. They looked like little, naked, skydiving mermaids. They smiled and waved to me as they drifted in my apartment straight through the window. Some landed on me, clinging to my sweater, others landed elsewhere around the room, wiggling crazily like fish out of water. I closed my eyes for a respite from the fishy incursion around me, but that didn't help. I saw all sorts of strangeness in the nothingness. There were colorful fractals, geometric patterns, pinball machines from hell, werewolves, wolpertingers, the occasional metamorphosing water elf. The Cheshire Cat came last, grinning at me from the far reaches of my imagination. I stared at that cat until all that was left of him was the grin, as one does.

The sound of laughter snapped me out of the trance.

THE IMAGINED HOMECOMING OF ICARUS ISAKOV

Opening my eyes, I saw the mermaids had left the party, but my guests hadn't. They were sitting around me in the living room, reading the signatures aloud from one of my old high school yearbooks. Someone must have plucked it from the bookshelf.

I sat up and listened. The guests passed the yearbook around, each reciting the signatures like they were poetry. Everyone found them highly entertaining, including me. I hadn't looked through that yearbook in years, so I was genuinely surprised at the contents. There was everything from the expectedly juvenile to the unexpectedly insane.

Icarus! You were the sweetest goblin in French class. Doux comme la merde licorn enrobee de sucre, excusez mon francais[5]. You must come over this summer. Like seriously. You must must must! We'll cook a cassoulet. K.I.T.

Icarus O'Icarus, your tootsie roll nipples stare straight through my soul like the eyes of a Chinese dragon. Talk does not cook rice. A fall in the ditch makes you wiser. All things change. And school sucks. Neptune nuts.

Some sign the front, some sign the back, I'm the

---

[5] *Sweet as sugar-coated unicorn shit, excuse my French.*

first to sign your crack.

Few things. It rains diamonds on Saturn. If you folded this yearbook page 42 times it would reach the moon. Shakespeare invented the name Jessica. You share 50% of your DNA with bananas. That is all. Good day.

Hey Man, Science was a blast. Not! Party hard this summer. Party hard forever. And ever and ever. Toke that peace pipe and remember me. Remember the good old days. Amen!

We read the signatures aloud, fascinated at the ridiculousness until we came to the very last signature. It was no ordinary yearbook signature. It was too long to be ordinary. It was more letter. It was one of those unexpected letters.

"Who's Ruby?" Someone asked, handing me the yearbook.

I read the letter to myself.

I saw you through your bedroom window last night. I caught myself staring as you were changing for bed. I tried to get your attention, but you closed your blinds before I could get it. If I still had it, I could have used that old tin can telephone we used to talk to each other with. You don't look out your window, at my window, as often as you used to. Anyway, I must have been thinking about you as I fell asleep because I dreamed about you. It was this doozy of a dream.

In the dream, we were little again. Well, we started little. We grew up as the dream went on. At first, we were playing pretend in the school gymnasium, under the parachute, in fairyland. Remember fairyland? We were running, jumping, and screaming all crazy-like until I collided with you. After that, the gymnasium became the Rollerway, and instead of running, we were all roller skating. The rink was busy, like it used to be. We skated a couple's skate together, and everyone stared at us because they wanted to be us. When the skate ended, the disco ball lights turned to snowflakes. All of a sudden, we were at the park, in a snowball fight. There were snow angels, floating over no man's land into the blizzard. We played there in the snow awhile, until a nightmare interrupted the dream. The Watchman! He chased us down Main Street, all the way through downtown, almost to the interstate, when Artie pulled up and rescued us in his Buick. He drove us straight into the river! We were driving down it like it was any old dirt road. You were next to me in the back seat, and we weren't little kids anymore. We looked like we do now. Artie played a certain song on the cassette player, one just for us. I kissed you and you kissed me, and I could feel the spray from the river water in my hair as we sped on to who knows where. I don't remember when the car disappeared, but it did, and it was just you and me, and maybe a mermaid, swimming in the river. We swam to shore and made our way through the woods to this meadow, where a Ferris wheel waited for us. As soon as we hopped on, the thing took off into the night sky like a hot air balloon. We floated over Rockville, talking and laughing, pointing out this or that below. Then it started raining, and we started dancing. We danced out of the carriage and into the rain like a couple of absolute lunatics! I was so busy dancing I didn't notice the rest of the world disappearing. Before it disappeared, I found you, or maybe you found me. I was sad at the world ending, but glad I was with you when it did.

I woke up all hot and bothered. The way we grew up in the dream made it seem like half our lives had passed in the middle of the night. Had they? From grade school to now doesn't seem such a long time, does it? I wonder how all that time passed by so quickly. It feels like it passes quicker every day.

They say to fly in your dreams means you're trying to escape or to be set free from something. I guess that makes sense because most of us are escaping Rockville soon. I wonder what's out there, out past the river, on the other side of the mountains. Whatever it is, I hope it doesn't change you. I hope it's not so great it makes you forget home. I hope you'll come back and remember with me. I hope you'll come back and imagine with me. We can imagine all we were, all we wanted to be. And when we're old-timers, we'll imagine ourselves young again, and it will be just like old times. We'll imagine and remember and be happy.

Your Pal,
Ruby

Acknowledgements

Thanks for reading. Hope you liked it. That story is less fantastical than it seemed. Many of the chapters are based on actual events. Artie *did* play the last cassette in his old Skylark, one summer night forever ago. I went night swimming, more than once. I played parachute games, fought snowball fights, and conjured monsters in mirrors. I drank memories in mystical bars. Thanks to all of you who were there with me.

Thanks to editor April Jones, for taking on such an unusual project, and making it better.

Thanks to the idea of home, first imagined my way by the one and only Rose Wiley. Thanks for all the homes, mom. Thanks for everything.

Last but not least, thanks to Kellan, Francesca, and Jenny. Our home is mythical.

Works Cited

Burnett, Frances. *A Little Princess*. United States: Charles Scribner's Sons, 1905.

The Carter Family. Weeping Willow. On The Carter Family: 1927-1934. Carter Family, 1927.

Hiraeth. Retrieved from: https://other-wordly.tumblr.com/post/33868390948/hiraeth

Idol, Billy. Dancing with Myself. On Don't Stop. Chrysalis, 1981.

King, Ben. There Goes My Baby. On There Goes My Baby. Atlantic, 1951.

Mercer, Johnny. Moon River. On Breakfast at Tiffany's. RCA, 1961.

Proust, Marcel. *In Search of Lost Time*. France: Grasset and Gallimard, 1913.

Steve Wiley, Author

Steve is a father, husband, uncle, brother, friend, and purveyor of speculative fantasy. He grew up in and around Chicagoland, where he still lives with his wife and two kids. He has been published in an array of strange and serious places, from the U.S. Chamber of Commerce in Washington, D.C., to *Crannóg* magazine in Galway, Ireland. His first novel, *The Fairytale Chicago of Francesca Finnegan*, was published in 2017. Steve has an undergraduate degree in something he has forgotten from Illinois State University and a graduate degree in something equally forgotten from DePaul University. Steve once passionately kissed a bronze seahorse in the middle of Buckingham Fountain. You can email Steve at Lavenderlinepress@gmail.com.

CPSIA information can be obtained
at www.ICGtesting.com
Printed in the USA
LVHW050728240523
747570LV00009B/76